Six Bullets Left

Barry Cord

G.K. Hall & Co. • Waterville, Maine

Published in 2001 by arrangement with Golden West Literary Agency.

G.K. Hall Large Print Paperback Series.

The text of this Large Print edition is unabridged.
Other aspects of the book may vary from the original edition.

Set in 16 pt. Plantin.

Printed in the United States on permanent paper.

Library of Congress Cataloging-in-Publication Data

Cord, Barry, 1913–
Six bullets left / Barry Cord.
p. cm.
ISBN 0-7838-9507-0 (lg. print : sc : alk. paper)
1. Texas Rangers — Fiction. 2. Texas — Fiction. 3. Large type books. I. Title.
PS3505.O6646 S54 2001
813′.54—dc21 2001024701

Six Bullets Left

I

Bob Crane came out of the desert, riding from something he couldn't see, hounded by a premonition he couldn't define. Where the long, deep shadow of Iron Butte reached out to the rim of the sandstone bluff he pulled to a stop, forcing himself to heed the mare's faltering stride.

But an odd and unshakable fear rode him, pinching his thin face. He felt it rise like panic in his throat and he brushed a damp strand of brown hair from his eyes, shifting with nervous impatience on the hard saddle.

A wind came off the long, dark places, brittle and dry as an old woman's reaching hand. . . . He closed his eyes, trying to blot out the nameless fear that haunted him.

He roused himself after a few moments and twisted to look back into the desert night. He saw nothing move. He heard nothing. But he reached under his leg for the carbine thrust in the saddle scabbard; held across his pommel, it gave off the slight warmth of reassurance.

Below and to the south of the bluff the spatter of Muleshoe's lights reached out a welcoming hand. He forced a small sigh of relief to his dry lips.

He had outrun them, after all!

He turned the tired mare away from the rim and rode down an old goat trail, across a wide arroyo separating Muleshoe from the desert, and pulled up again before a long adobe building on the edge of Gila Road.

The law office was dark, which told him that Marshal Tom Benton was out making his rounds. Disappointment rode a hard spur through Crane. He turned and put a nervous glance on the dark trail behind him.

The Llano Escalante was a mysterious sea shimmering in the starlight. There was a quality to the desert night that deceived the eye; it made a man strain to glimpse the far places, the thicker shadows, the movements that were only in his panicky mind.

The wind, thick with sand now, lifted from the far reaches of this desolate land, rolled like a ground fog toward town. The grit stung Crane's face.

He was a small, slight man, thin-cheeked, stoop-shouldered. He was carelessly dressed — old pair of pants, blue shirt open at his throat. He wasn't wearing a hat, a foolhardy idiosyncrasy in this country of blazing sunlight. He was careful to foster this appearance of vague incompetence. In Muleshoe he was known as a tenderfoot Easterner who had come west for his health. A man who washed dishes and did the chores in the Eldorado Hotel and amused himself and the hotel's dining-room guests by scribbling humorous or romantic verse on menu cards.

He had played his role well, but it had finally caught up with him. He knew he had little time left. Too little time to get word back to his home office. His only hope lay with the town marshal.

He edged the mare in close to the adobe building and the open side window caught his attention, shaping his next move. Instinctively he cast another glance into the desert. The sky was getting murky, blotting out distance. But he wasn't reassured. He had blundered this last time out and he knew he would be given no other chance.

He reached in his pocket for the knife he carried. The note he had written and tied around the knife rustled under his fingers. He had arranged for just such an emergency when he knew he had been seen. He flung the knife through the open window, heard it hit and slide across the floor. Then he kneed the mare away from the dark building and headed for the main part of town.

He rode down Muleshoe's main street and it was like riding into a ghost town. Most of the shops had wooden shutters closed against the wind off the Escalante and only occasionally did a weak light probe the murky night.

He turned into the livery stable a block from the hotel, and, having reached this far, the man called Crane felt the stir of hope that he might have shaken the implacable pursuers from the desert.

The hostler took charge of the mare with a sigh of relief. "The desert's no place for a sick man to be riding," he said worriedly. "I was afraid you'd gone and got lost." He ran a familiar hand over the mare's sweat-crusted shoulder. "Been gone since this morning. And she looks like she's been ridden hard."

Crane forced an apologetic smile to his lips. He looked his thirty years only when he smiled — at other times his thin, worried features seemed older.

"Rode out to Purple Butte," he confessed. "Tired me out. Found some shade and — heck, I fell asleep. Was near sundown when I woke. I tried to beat the storm into town."

The hostler accepted the explanation. "Good thing you made it in before it got real bad out there. I was getting plumb worried about you."

Crane slipped an extra dollar into the hostler's palm. "I learned my lesson," he said soberly. "Next time I'll stay close by."

He left the stable and walked the block to the hotel, bucking the gritty wind. He met no one on the walk, although in front of the Oro Grande Saloon a pair of hipshot horses tailed the wind. They looked tired, as though they had been ridden far — and recently.

He quickened his step. The Eldorado loomed three stories above him, its shadow enclosing him, bringing a sense of security. In another minute he would pass through that closed door, safe at last. A sigh of thankfulness escaped his tight-pressed lips.

The faded wooden sign creaked mournfully as he went up the steps. The wide veranda fronting the hotel was dark and deserted, the chairs leaning like mute spectators against the wall.

Crane paused with his hand on the knob of the heavy oak door, composing his features before entering.

The arrow made no sound. It came out of the night, from across the street, driven with terrific force. It hit him between his shoulder blades and went completely through him, burying its iron head deep in the plank door.

The slight man's body twitched and jerked in silent agony, and finally stilled. The tough hickory shaft held his weight, like a butterfly pinned to a board.

He was still there, nailed grotesquely to the door, when Mrs. Amy Rankin, coming to pick up the hotel wash, saw him.

There was a lagging moment before the horror penetrated her slow mind and was translated into a high, prolonged shriek of terror. . . .

II

Town Marshal Tom Benton found the body surrounded by a small cluster of silent, uncomfortable men. Phil Petersen, editor of the *Muleshoe Chronicle*, helped him free Crane's body and bring it into the lobby.

They laid Crane out on one of the leather-covered settees and Benton stood over him, feeling the dryness forming in his mouth, giving his tongue a cottony texture. He was a grizzled man in his late forties, and he had been a lawman most of his life. Fear was something he had always been able to control. But it was getting away from him now. . . .

Petersen, a tall, stringy man about the marshal's age, was holding the short, blunt-headed arrow in his hands. Frowning, he turned to Benton with a worried snap: "Ever see anything like this before, Tom?"

Benton shook his head. The arrow bore no resemblance to any he had ever seen, nor could he imagine the bow which had driven it with such terrific force.

Petersen swore. "Who did it, Tom? What are we going to do about — about him?"

The marshal offered no answer. He had come

to the point where he trusted no one, not even himself. In a gathering sense of disaster, he had taken it upon himself to write for help to Ranger headquarters; it was his third letter to that office and he had the dismal feeling that this one, like the others, would be ignored.

Back in Austin, seven hundred miles from the Escalante, the idea of the Baron was a joke, his claims the pretensions of a madman, his threats laughed at. But all along the Llano Escalante the threat of the Baron was grimly real.

The newspaper publisher ran lean fingers through his iron-gray hair. The unruly mop gave him the appearance of a lean terrier. His eyes were a bright blue.

"They've got us frightened to death!" he said angrily, bitterly. "Not only us, but every town bordering the desert. They raid as they please, and they kill as they wish, with seeming impunity —"

The marshal turned away. He knew from past experience that when the *Chronicle* publisher was aroused he'd be the target of the man's ire, of his unreasoning denunciations.

"Wait a minute, Tom!" Petersen's voice was harsh. "You've been avoiding me lately. Is it a guilty conscience?"

Benton paused. He was near the door. The men between him and the newspaperman looked uneasy.

"You told me you wrote to Ranger headquarters for help," Petersen added. He looked bitter and frustrated, standing there, an angry man seeking a solution. "I don't want to sound unreasonable, Tom. But where are they?"

The marshal gave him a stony look, then shrugged heavy shoulders. He didn't bother to reply. He opened the door and stepped out onto the dark porch. He faced the murky shadows across the street and felt his skin crawl.

Petersen's accusation weighed on him. He knew how the man felt about the Rangers — more than once he had attacked the organization which most Texas men held in high esteem. He and Petersen had broken on this issue, but he had to admire the man's integrity of viewpoint. Petersen had taken his stand and he had stuck by it.

He walked toward his office, but stopped off at the Butte View Lunch where his niece Ruth worked. Sam Dillman, his brother-in-law, pushed a mug of coffee across the counter to him.

"Have your supper yet, Tom?"

The marshal shook his head. "Not hungry," he muttered. He turned on his stool as Ruth came into the lunchroom, a shawl covering her head. She shook sand from it as she came to the counter.

"I just heard about Bob Crane," she said quickly. "Such a horrible way to die!"

Tom Benton took a sip of his coffee. His face was drawn. "The whole thing's too much for me to handle, Sam," he said to the man across the counter. "It's not my job, anyway. I've tried to tell George Vollmer that. He's got twenty-five thousand dollars in his office safe he's afraid to move out of town on the stage. He wants *me* to be responsible." The marshal made a wry face.

Sam said earnestly, "Chuck it, Tom. Let them hire another man, if they can."

Benton made a tired gesture.

"Tom, there ain't another man in the county who'd touch this job," Sam growled. "And they know it, too. Vollmer, Petersen, Amos Selwick —" Sam's lips curled. "You'd think they run this town —"

"Don't they?" Benton's voice was remote; he was looking moodily down into his cup.

"No more than the rest of us," Sam snapped angrily. "And they're just as scared as we are of what's out there . . ."

"I've done what I can," Tom said. He pushed his cup from him. "I've written to Ranger headquarters. I've even mailed a letter to the governor." He laughed shortly. "You know what probably happened to them, Sam. Gave somebody a great big laugh."

Sam shrugged. Ruth said quietly, "You've done what you can, Uncle Tom. Perhaps even the Rangers wouldn't do more."

"I don't know," Tom replied. "I asked for Jackson, if he was available. The Ranger they called Solitary."

Sam was refilling his cup. He shook his head, as if annoyed. "The Ranger who gunned Red

Owens in that Salt River cleanup? The man Phil Petersen calls a bounty hunter?"

Tom pushed the cup away and stood up. "I'm not trying to please Petersen," he said flatly. "I don't know what kind of a man Jackson is. But he's a Ranger. And that's good enough for me."

Sam said disgustedly, "Fine, Tom. That'll work out just fine in Muleshoe —" He tossed his apron under the counter and stalked away, disappearing through a side door.

Tom grinned sourly. He was almost at the door when Ruth called after him, "I'll bring you a tray later on, Uncle Tom."

He nodded, giving her a tired smile. . . .

Benton found the note tacked on his front door. It was too dark to read it. He tore it loose and brought it inside the office, pausing to lock the door behind him. He was aware that he had left a window open, and he closed it and drew the shade before lighting the lamp on his desk.

The message he held in his fist was blunt: *You're next, Marshal.*

He felt the fear crawl down his spine as he read it. He crumpled the note in his fist, flung it on the desk and wheeled grimly for the gun rack against the south wall. He stepped on a hard object as he reached for the double-barreled shotgun and, looking down, he saw the knife Bob Crane had thrown through the window.

For a moment the meaning of it eluded him. He stared down dumbly at the pocketknife, his big hands clenched around the shotgun. Then he bent down and picked up the knife and brought it under the lamplight on the desk. Propping the shotgun against the desk side, he unknotted the string that held the note to the knife and spread the missive out under the lamp.

Smoothing the creases out with a horny palm, he scowled at the penciled block letters that at first made no sense to him.

Go east, young man, go east,
Into the land of emptiness;
Where the stars shine bright
And the binnacle light
Beckons to the lone wanderer.

Go west, young man, go west
To the rock of the skull,
And then south as the harpoon points. . . .

The strange message ended there, as though the writer had been interrupted. The marshal read the cryptic lines half a dozen times, trying to make sense out of them, trying to imagine who might have written this.

Bob Crane?

The Easterner wrote jingles and verse, and some of his work had appeared in the *Chronicle*, written in the same style as these lines. But if Crane had written this, what did it mean? Why had he taken this method of getting a message to him?

Had Crane been killed because of this? The

possibility turned the marshal's worried thoughts to the man who had been killed less than an hour ago.

Go west, young man, go west. . . .

Tom Benton pulled his can of tobacco to him and thoughtfully began filling his pipe. The words in front of him could make sense only if Bob Crane was not what he had seemed to be. They made sense only if somehow Bob Crane had found out what was out there in the Llano Escalante.

He heard the approach of a rider then, drumming faintly above the gritty whisper of the wind, and his next motions were instinctive. He folded Crane's note into a small square and buried it in the tobacco in the tin on his desk. Then he blew out the light, picked up the shotgun and turned to the door.

The rider pulled up in front. Benton waited in the dark, feeling the blood pound in his ears. He heard a horse blow heavily, and bit irons jingled in the night.

"Marshal!" The voice was direct, questioning.

Benton sucked in a harsh breath. What in the devil was he afraid of? He cursed his fear and walked to the door. Drawing the bolt, he swung the door wide and stood just to one side of it, hidden by the darkness within the office. Under his horny thumb the shotgun hammers clicked softly.

Murky starlight showed him the dark bulk of a rangy man sitting the saddle of a big black horse with a blaze face. A star glittered dimly from the man's coat — a star set in a gleaming silver circle.

Tom Benton recognized that symbol of Ranger authority. Relief welled up in him, making his voice thin as he stepped through the doorway.

"Ranger, I'm sure glad to see you!"

The man on the black horse eyed him with quiet appraisal. His face was a vague blur under his hat.

"You Marshal Tom Benton?"

Benton nodded.

"I'm Jackson," the stranger said. "Some folks call me Solitary."

"Jackson!" Benton drew a long breath. "I've never met you, Ranger. But I was never happier to see a man." He made a gesture toward his office. "Come inside. I've got a lot to tell you."

"What about?"

Benton paused in the act of turning. "About what's out there in the desert." His mouth twisted harshly. "I've seen a lot of strange things in my day, Jackson. But the bunch out there —"

"You know what's out there, eh?" The man's voice was probing.

"I've got a pretty good idea," Benton admitted. "It's been growing. And thanks to a feller named Bob Crane, I've got an idea where to look —"

He saw the thin reflection from the man's Colt as it came out of holster, but the implication behind the motion lagged in his head. He stood in the doorway, frowning. And then he saw the muzzle come up, and he made a belated effort to swing his shotgun up.

The rider's bullet dropped him limply across the threshold.

The black snorted and jumped at the muzzle blast close to its ear, and the gunman cursed him as his second shot went wild. He was trying to steady the black for another shot when the girl, coming to the office with a loaded tray, screamed.

The killer whirled the black horse around and dug spurs into the sleek flanks. He was a shadow lost in the darkness beyond the arroyo when Ruth reached the side of her uncle and knelt beside him.

III

Ten days later the first of two strangers to arrive in Muleshoe stepped from the morning stage and checked in at the Eldorado. He was a man of medium height, of stocky, muscular build and not more than twenty-five years old. He wore a flat-crowned black hat over shaggy straw hair, and the square-jawed, freckled face had an insolent cast.

He wore a long black coat over a gunbelt and holster, and the name he penned on the hotel register was Marvey Holt.

The hotel clerk was a tall sinewy-necked man who maintained an avid interest in all the Eldorado's guests. He read the name, and, because it stirred a familiar chord in his long memory, he said, "Staying with us long, Mr. Holt?"

The stranger was turning away from the desk when the question came; he turned and surveyed the clerk with candid regard. "Depends," he murmured.

The clerk's curiosity remained unblunted. "Muleshoe is kinda out of the way, now that the Santa Fe built that spur through to the county seat. What with the trouble we been having, we don't get many strangers here any more." His smile was a come-on.

Holt scratched the lobe of his left ear. "Sort of came prepared for trouble," he said coldly. His eyes had an icy directness as they met the clerk's. "I'm looking for a gent who goes by the name of Bob Crane."

The clerk swallowed hard and the smile left his face. "Bob Crane?" he echoed weakly.

"Heard he worked here," Holt said. He was facing the desk, but out of the corner of his eye he saw one of the loungers in the lobby get up and head for the door, and a glint came and vanished in his gaze.

"He did," the clerk said. He licked his lips, somehow oddly unnerved by this man with the familiar name which he could not quite place. "You — you'll find him in Boot Hill, at the end of Desert Avenue."

He saw no emotion in that insolent, freckled face. But Holt's voice was softer, asking its question: "When did it happen?"

"Ten days ago. Right outside this door —" The clerk swept his arm across the desk. He mumbled a version of what had happened to Bob Crane. "They got the marshal the same night," he concluded. "They just missed killing him, but the result is the same. Tom Benton ain't the same man —"

"They?" Holt's voice cut through the clerk's explanation.

"The Escalante raiders," the clerk said. His voice dropped and his eyes made their instinctive search of the lobby. "The Baron's men."

Holt nodded, as though this was sufficient explanation. He picked up his key and his bag. His smile had a cold twist to it. "Reckon I'll be staying a bit longer than I expected," he said, and went up to his room.

He remained just long enough to wash and change his shirt. When he came back through the lobby the clerk was no longer behind the desk. The fact made its impression on him, but did not bother him.

He stepped outside and oriented himself, a cool, somehow dangerous man paused on the top of the hotel steps. Desert Avenue ran south to the desert and in the slanting sun he saw the wooden markers dotting the sand hill at the end of town.

It took him ten minutes to reach the desolate cemetery baking under the high sun and only a few moments to find the new grave, piled with rocks to keep nocturnal prowlers from digging in the soft sand. The flat wooden headboard bore the painted information:

BOB CRANE
Died June 11, 1887

A tin can, bright with daffodils, was wedged among the rocks. He looked at it, wondering who had thought enough of the dead man to remember him this way. He was silent in the sun, his thoughts going back a long way both in time and distance. Then he heard the whirr of wheels as they crossed the sand in the arroyo and he was in Muleshoe again, standing by his brother's grave.

He didn't turn — although he heard the vehicle come up the hill road and stop close behind him — until a high, raspy voice asked, "Friend of yours, stranger?"

Holt stepped back and turned to the buggy which had driven up behind him. Two men sat on the spring seat. The driver was a tall, stringy sort of man with a shock of wild iron-gray hair and bright blue eyes. He was wearing a black coat and hat similar to Holt's, but the resemblance ended there. He had a quick, nervous way about him, and he repeated his question with rising impatience.

Marvey Holt shrugged. "Why?"

"I'm Phil Petersen," the driver snapped. "Publisher of the *Muleshoe Chronicle.*" He didn't introduce the hard-faced man beside him, but Marvey Holt knew a hired gunhand when he saw one.

He took a cigar from his breast pocket, bit off one end, and put it between his teeth. "You looking for news?" His voice held a mocking insolence.

"I'm after information," Petersen replied. "You asked about Crane at the hotel. Was he a friend of yours?"

"Maybe. Maybe not." Holt's eyes narrowed. "Why?"

"You stepped off the stage a half-hour ago," Petersen pointed out. "And the first thing you ask is about Bob Crane. You tell me why, stranger."

"Might be he owed me five bucks and I came to collect," Holt replied coldly. "I don't figure it's any of your business, Petersen. Not even if you were the law — and I don't happen to see a badge on you. Or on your scowling friend, either."

The gunman sitting alongside the *Chronicle* publisher leaned forward in the seat, a lean and watchful look tightening his horselike features.

Petersen's fingers closed over his forearm. "Let it pass, Nick. We want no trouble with him." He turned to Holt. "I asked you a civil question, son. There's been a lot of trouble around here lately. And maybe more to come. I think you can understand my interest in any stranger who comes to Muleshoe and asks questions about a man recently murdered."

Holt nodded slightly. "You asked the questions, pop. But I'll hold on to the answers."

Anger pushed its dark tide into Petersen's face. He studied Holt with bright regard, his lips sucking in against his store teeth. "All right, son," he said. "Just don't step too wide or too fast while you're in town. That's a warning."

Holt watched him swing the buggy around, head down the hill. His hand brushed against his Colt butt as he reached in his pocket for a match.

"I warned you you were playing out of your

class, Bob," he murmured. "But you wouldn't listen. . . ."

The second stranger rode into Muleshoe along no beaten trail. He appeared at the edge of town in midafternoon, with the sun hot against his dusty shoulders. He had come from the direction of Iron Butte rising like a black gnarled fist southwest of town.

He was a tall man with a wide spread of shoulders tapering down to a rider's narrow waist and hips. The brass shells in his cartridge belts glinted in the sunlight; the pair of Peacemaker Colts in thonged-down holsters had an unobtrusive deadliness. His was a strong, dark face drawn into sober lines by a thousand lonely trails and his eyes reflected his aloneness in their cold and noncommittal appraisal.

He was a man who stood out, alone or in a crowd, a solitary man by nature, more at home in the hard and violent reaches of Texas than in Austin.

He crossed the arroyo by the goat path Bob Crane had taken ten days earlier, and the first building he came to was the law office, casting its thin edge of shade across the widening road. The sign over the door read, *Marshal's Office,* and the stranger took this in before letting his gaze rest on the stoop-shouldered man sitting on the bench by the door.

Bandages showed under the man's worn hat and pain had carved recent lines in the man's leathery face. He stood with head bowed, just within the narrow line of shade. He was whittling with absent concentration on a hunk of soft pine.

The stranger reined his roan in a few paces from the whittler and leaned forward, resting his forearms on his saddle. He could see that the man was whittling a wooden Colt. The stranger dropped his gaze to the empty holster on the man's thigh, and it occurred to him that a wooden gun made a poor substitute.

He waited in the hot sun, but the whittler either hadn't noticed him or was intent on ignoring him.

"I'm looking for Tom Benton," the stranger said. His voice held a patient softness.

Benton's head came up. His eyes searched the rider's face with a vacant look. He wiped his mouth with the back of his hand, grinned fatuously.

"Howdy," he said.

The rider frowned. "You the marshal of Muleshoe?"

Benton's right hand lifted to his shirt; his fingers fumbled aimlessly. "Marshal?" His hand moved on to his face and a puzzled look came into his eyes.

"You sent for me," the rider said slowly. "Don't you remember?"

Benton looked up. His eyes were dark and tortured with the effort of remembering. A light seemed to probe through the murk of forgetfulness; it faded. He licked his lips. "Can't remember —" he mumbled. He ran the balls of his fingers across his forehead. "Who are you?"

"The name's Jackson," Solitary said. "Texas Ranger."

The name produced an instant reaction in the older man. He jerked back and raised his arm in front of his face, as if he were expecting a blow. A strangled cry came from his lips. Then he lunged to his feet, jammed his shoulder against the closed door. His fingers clawed at the latch. He disappeared inside.

Solitary frowned. He had come a long way at this man's request for help; he couldn't understand the man's actions.

He heard a girl's voice call, and he turned his attention up the road to the first cluster of buildings making up Muleshoe.

A girl was hurrying toward him. He could see her face, white in the sun, and the urgency in her voice surprised him.

"Leave him alone!"

Solitary shrugged. He swung out of saddle, stepping down away from the law office. The move saved his life.

The marshal appeared in the doorway with a shotgun. He had the muzzle tilted up just as the Ranger dismounted — the shotgun blast went high over the roan's saddle.

The animal jerked away from the heavy explosion. Solitary whirled, took three quick strides which brought him up against the adobe wall.

His right-hand Colt came up just as Benton's muzzle made its sharp-swinging arc to follow him.

He heard the girl scream as he fired. He aimed for the shotgun, but his slug ricocheted off the barrel and tore a bad gash in Benton's forearm.

The marshal dropped the shotgun. He crouched in the doorway like a cornered animal, his eyes wild. And then Ruth Dillman came between him and the Ranger.

IV

Solitary Jackson stepped away from the building side. He had acted instinctively to save his life. Now, as his shadow moved across this girl, a frown filtered across the hardness of his face.

Benton was huddled against the door frame, the shotgun lying at his feet. He was clutching his injured arm and staring over the girl's shoulder, like a boy who expects to be whipped.

"Leave him alone!" the girl cried shrilly.

Jackson eased his Colt into holster and made a pacifying gesture. "I didn't want to hurt him, ma'am," he said gently. "He tried to kill me. I think you saw that."

She nodded. "He's been hurt. Uncle Tom doesn't always know what he's doing —"

"Said he was a Ranger," Benton broke in. His voice held the inflection of an odd hate. He looked at Jackson with narrowing eyes; his unshaved face had a slack, confused look. "He came to kill me, Ruth. Like the other feller —"

Ruth took him by the arm. "No. He won't hurt you —"

A crowd was beginning to collect around them. A harried-looking man in shirtsleeves broke through that group and came to stand beside Ruth. He turned and faced the Ranger with a belligerent scowl, an old-model Dragoon pistol in his hand.

"What's happened, Ruth?" Sam Dillman asked. "This hombre looking for trouble?"

The irony of the situation brought a bleak frown to Jackson's eyes. He had come a long way at Marshal Tom Benton's request; this was a strange way, he thought, to be greeted.

"I reckon there's been a slight misunderstanding," he said drily. "I came to town on official business. I'm a Ranger."

"Ranger?" Sam's eyes held a puzzled glint. He turned to his daughter. "Did Tom try to —"

She nodded. "Uncle Tom made a mistake. He tried to kill this man —"

"Kill who? What's going on?" Phil Petersen's voice had a sharply authoritative ring as he pushed through the sullen crowd. Nick was with him.

He was bareheaded, as though the disturbance here, at the edge of town, had pulled him away from his work. He looked more like a preacher than a newspaper publisher, or maybe it was because there was a little of both in the man. He turned to face Jackson, his voice brusque and demanding: "Who are you? What do you want here?"

Jackson eased back against the building and studied this man, the hostile faces flanking him. They were waiting for his answer with a sullen expectancy, and it occurred to him that Muleshoe was a town ridden by trouble and that all strangers were suspect. He could see little gain in keeping his identity from them, though he had not come to Muleshoe with this in mind.

"I'm a Ranger," he said. "I'm here on official business."

Petersen stiffened. "Ranger? You can prove that?"

"If I have to." Jackson's voice was flat. He stood apart from them, his own manner changing, becoming remote. He was a man best left alone. He was uncomfortable in towns — too many people depressed him. Environment shaped him; he moved through a land that at best still smoldered with violence. On the wrong side of the law he could have been one of the three most wanted men in Texas — it was this quality in him that made some men call him bounty hunter.

The *Chronicle* publisher sensed this in the tall, quiet man. He turned to the crowd. "All right, break it up!" He had a domineering way about him, a highhandedness born of some inner sense of authority. Perhaps it was abetted by the presence of the sneering gunman at his side.

He turned to face Ruth and her father. "You'd better take Tom home," he snapped. "And keep him locked up! I'm closing this office until we can get another marshal."

Tom Benton tried to get by Ruth. "I'm still marshal of Muleshoe," he protested. He lifted his bloody hand to his temple and fingered the bandage. His voice trailed away as if he was suddenly unsure of himself. "I am still marshal . . ."

"Sure you are, Tom!" Sam Dillman growled, eyeing Petersen with open hostility. "But we've got to get you over to Doc Harrigan's office. You need medical attention."

Benton allowed himself to be led away. The crowd began to break up, straggling back up the street. Ruth paused to look back at the Ranger.

"He didn't know what he was doing," she said. "Please believe that."

Jackson shrugged. "I'm not holding it against him," he said levelly. "I'd like to come around, later, and talk with him. Maybe I can convince him I'm not out to kill him."

The girl nodded. "Please do. Later."

Benton shook his head violently and tried to break away. The girl held on tightly and Sam Dillman put his stocky body against his brother-in-law's. Together they walked a reluctant Tom Benton up the street.

Phil Petersen walked to the doorway and picked up the shotgun Benton had dropped. He disappeared inside the law office with it, returning the weapon to its place in the gun rack.

When he came to the door the waning sun was in his face, outlining with harsh clarity the deep arrogant lines grooving his mouth.

"I'm Philip Petersen, publisher of the *Muleshoe Chronicle*," he introduced himself. "This is Nick Cates."

Jackson's glance brushed the cold-eyed gunman. Cates was regarding him with professional appraisal, and a bleak curiosity stirred in the big Ranger.

"You claim to be a Ranger?" Petersen's tone held a cool skepticism.

"I am," the big man said. "The name's Jackson."

A murmur went through the remaining crowd. Petersen frowned. Nick Cates's gaze narrowed speculatively and a remote antagonism tightened his lips.

"Oh, yes," Petersen said. "The Ranger they call Solitary —" He glanced around the crowd. "Where are the others?"

"I came alone," Jackson said.

Nick sneered. "He's a big man, Mr. Petersen. The Baron doesn't scare him!"

"Does he scare you?" Jackson's voice was bleak with anger.

"I'm not looking for him," Cates replied.

"Shut up, Nick!" Petersen ordered. His voice was dispassionate. He made a quick gesture to the Ranger. "If you're Jackson, I've been expecting you. Tom Benton said he sent for you."

Jackson nodded.

"He did it against my orders," Petersen snapped. "One Ranger — or a dozen — won't do much good out here. No offense intended, Jackson."

The Ranger's eyes held a remote cynicism. "That bad, eh?"

"Worse," Petersen growled. He made a gesture up the street. "No sense in standing around out here, Solitary. Come on down to my office. I'll let you know what you'll be in for."

The *Chronicle* faced the Eldorado Hotel at an angle across the dusty width of the main street. It was a two-story brick building with outside stairs leading to living quarters above the shop.

Show windows flanked the door, each of which carried the lettered information:

THE CHRONICLE
The Voice of the Escalante
Philip Petersen, Publisher

The man working at the type cases was short and dumpy. He turned a slack, whisky-puffed face to Jackson as the Ranger followed Nick and Philip Petersen into the shop. He had the lack-luster eyes of a man just getting over a drunk, and showed little interest as Petersen introduced him.

"This is Red Casey," the publisher said. "Best typesetter west of the Mississippi — when he's sober. Which," he said ominously, "isn't often enough."

They went on into a small office partitioned off at the rear of the shop. Cates waited in the doorway, a lean, alert man making a pretense of casualness.

"Nick," Petersen said, turning, "get Elias Woods to put a new lock on the door of the marshal's office. I'll see that Sam keeps his brother-in-law away from there."

Cates shrugged, laid a lingering glance on Jackson, and went out. Petersen motioned to the Ranger to take a chair, and eased down into the swivel seat behind the desk.

"We've been humoring Tom, since he got that bullet in his skull," he explained caustically. "Let him sit around in the sun and pretend he's still marshal. Didn't think he'd go crazy at the first stranger to show up."

Jackson smiled humorlessly. "What happened to Benton?"

Petersen started to say something, then eased back in his chair, a cautious look crossing his face. "Just a minute, fella. I heard you call yourself Jackson, the Ranger most people know as Solitary. But I haven't seen any identification."

"Fair enough," Jackson said. He reached in his coat, brought out his wallet and laid it on Petersen's desk. The bright badge of Texas authority was pinned to the inside flap — a silver star set in a gleaming circle of silver.

Petersen pushed it back. "You're Jackson," he admitted. "But like I told you, Benton had no authority calling in the Rangers. I told him he was making a mistake. This thing out here in the Escalante is too big. That's why I wrote to the governor myself —"

"Just what is the trouble out here?" Jackson interrupted drily.

"Didn't Tom explain it?"

"Some of it. Something about a bunch of bronco Apaches raiding out of the Escalante. Mentioned a crackpot who calls himself the Baron who's declared himself head of a new state he calls Deserta —"

"Crackpot!" Petersen came forward in his chair, his eyes blazing. "Tom Benton is a fool! He didn't realize just what we're up against, out here! He — Just a minute. I've got something to show you."

Jackson waited as Petersen pushed back and fumbled around in a lower drawer. The man brought up a rolled poster which he flattened out on the desk in front of the Ranger.

"Ever see this before?"

Solitary got up and read the printed proclamation.

NOTICE

This land has seceded from the State of Texas and hereafter comes within the jurisdiction of the new State of Deserta. All trespassers will be given ten days to clear out. Those who remain will pay taxes to representatives of the new State. Violators will be shot. Trespassers without the signed permission of the new State will be treated as enemies of the State and will be dealt with according to the laws of Deserta.

THE BARON.

"These posters have been put up all along the

Escalante," Petersen said. "A half-dozen small ranchers have been burned out — three others just abandoned their places. Crowley's GC spread, over by Iron Butte, had two men butchered and its linehouse burned out."

Jackson frowned. "When did this start?"

"We started hearing rumors about the Baron last year," Petersen growled. "Shortly after I came to Muleshoe. Some folks around here claim they saw him, before he went into the desert." Petersen shrugged. "I'm a newspaperman. I listen to all stories, but I only believe half what I hear, and I don't trust anything I don't see myself. Like most of us, I thought he was some harmless crank, looking for a little notoriety. We're out on the edge of nothing out here — you'd be surprised the kind of people come through Muleshoe."

He got up and walked to a small cabinet beside a wooden file and took out a bottle of Scotch and two glasses. He seemed a little puzzled about something.

"Didn't Tom write you anything about the Baron?"

Solitary shook his head. "Only what I told you. I reckon he intended to tell me what he knew when I saw him."

Petersen poured. He had a nervous hand, but he was generous with his liquor.

"Tom Benton is a fool," he said flatly. "Oh, he was a good enough town marshal — didn't scare easy and could handle a gun well enough to take care of the usual trouble. Now —" Petersen shrugged callously — "maybe he'd be better off if that bullet had killed him."

Jackson appraised this man, wondering what had been the relationship between Petersen and the town marshal. "Sounds like you two didn't get along," he said.

Petersen took a swallow of his Scotch and put his glass down with a slight grimace. It occurred to Jackson that the newspaper publisher was not a drinking man, that he kept his whisky on hand for company only.

"Tom is a close-mouthed idiot!" Petersen snapped. "He wouldn't listen to me at all. I told him this thing was big. That this Baron was crazy — *is* crazy — like a fox! But he preferred to work with that Easterner, Bob Crane."

"Crane?" Jackson's voice was curious. "Benton didn't mention working with anyone here."

A glint of annoyance passed through Petersen's eyes. "I'm just guessing," he said. "Tom was shot the same night Bob Crane was killed. I just sort of connected them —" He saw the look on the Ranger's face and he added harshly: "I might as well fill you in as to what happened the night Tom Benton was shot."

Solitary listened. Listening to trouble was part of his job. But he couldn't make the connection Petersen had, not from the publisher's story. He could see no reason for Crane's death, not if the man was what he had appeared to be during his stay in Muleshoe.

"Bob Crane was killed by an arrow," Petersen ended. "No one knows for sure, but the Baron is rumored to head a bunch of renegade whites and sorehead Chiricahuas. Some of the killings look like the work of Apaches. But take a look at this!"

He walked to the filing cabinet and took an arrow lying behind a ledger. "I'm no authority on Indians or arrows," Petersen growled, "but this doesn't look like any arrow used by Indians around here."

Solitary examined the short shaft. It had an almost blunt iron head, a hardwood shaft, a few chicken feathers to guide it. The iron head was partially flattened and the shaft was stained brown.

"This arrow went clean through Bob Crane and into two inches of oak planking," Petersen said.

Something about that arrow nagged at Jackson. It was too short for one thing. A man couldn't draw back far enough, even on a sixty-pound bow, to give much penetrating power to this arrow. And the iron head was fitted on, capping the shaft. No Indian he knew of was capable of this type of machined fitting.

An odd weapon to use, he thought grimly. And the trouble here took on new proportions.

Tom Benton's letter, blunt and misspelled, had carried a tangible fear. It had been addressed to Captain MacDonald, head of the Texas Rangers in Austin.

DEAR CAPTAIN MACDONALD:

I aint much of a hand at writin. Ive bin a peace officer most of my life an I dont scare easy. But we ben havin trouble here. Holdups. Killins. Cant seem to pin down whose behind it. I keep hearin rumers of a jasper who calls himself the Baron. Hes got a tough bunch with him an he holes out somewhere in the Lano Escalante. I think the mans crazy. He claims the desert and the range borderin it belongs to him. Hes posted signs all along Sand Creek. Ill show them to your man when he comes. If you can send that troubleshooter of yours, the one they call Solitary, Id feel a lot easier. Ill be waitin for him, or for some word from you.

This is the third letter I wrote you. Im gettin despirit. . . .

Jackson put the arrow back on the desk and got to his feet. "Maybe the trouble you've got here is bigger than I can handle, Petersen," he said evenly. "But I'm here and I'll take a crack at it. And to make things official, I'll take over Benton's job until you, or whoever has the authority here, gets a new lawman to take Tom's place."

Petersen shook his head. "I've got nothing against you, Jackson. Not personally. There's been rumors that you're a killer hiding behind that badge, even that you're a bounty hunter —" He held up a hand as Jackson's eyes glinted. "Just a minute, Ranger. I didn't say I believed that. But I want to make it clear that Tom

Benton sent for you, against my advice, and that of most of the influential people in this town. We think you'll be making a mistake staying here. This Baron's playing a game too big for you, or for anyone but the state militia —"

"I was sent down here to look into that," Jackson cut in drily. "I'll be the judge of whether we need an army down here."

The annoyance spread across Petersen's deep-lined face; his eyes held the thin gleam of malevolence. "I know you've got a reputation to uphold, Jackson. But this time you're over-reaching yourself." He spread his hands in a pacifying gesture. "Look — the governor's due here next week. This is an election year; he is making a political tour through this part of the state anyway. I wrote I wanted to see him about this trouble we've been having. I got word from his secretary that he'd come through Muleshoe on his swing north."

He leaned back in his swivel chair and made an attempt at a friendly smile. "Let the governor deal with this, Jackson. Secession comes under the head of treason, doesn't it?"

The big Ranger ignored the question. "I'll see what I can do until the governor shows up." His smile had an iron quality that reached back into the depths of his yellow-flecked eyes. "The Rangers, too, are interested in this character who wants a part of Texas to secede from the Union."

V

Nick Cates's long shadow fell across the stubby carpenter who was putting a new lock on the law office door. The gunman had just come out of the building where he had made one more tour of inspection. The dusty interior, he observed, was about the way it had been the night Tom Benton was shot.

He heard the rider approaching and he turned, his long face growing curious and yet remote. He had heard stories about this big man, and a pulse of excitement brought a watchful glitter to his eyes.

He stepped away from the man working on the lock, his right thumb coming up to hook carelessly in his cartridge-studded belt.

Solitary came to a stop a few paces from the law office. The day was dying. There was a dull haze over the desert, like a low fog bank rolling in toward Muleshoe. In the town itself the air was still; the heat of the day had a breathless quality.

Elias Woods stopped working on the lock and glanced at Jackson. His attention was caught by the Ranger's narrowing frown; he turned and looked helplessly at Nick, sensing the tension whipsawing around him.

"Keep working, Elias!" Nick's voice was harsh.

Elias licked his lips. He had a hammer and a chisel in his hands, but suddenly they became clumsy tools over which he had little control.

Solitary rested his hands on the pommel. He could feel the push of Nick's challenging stare and he knew that the long-faced gunman was set for trouble.

He shifted slightly and put his glance along the sandy street to the beginning of the business block where men were grouping in small knots on the walks. The scent of trouble was all through town, but the watchers were keeping their distance.

It puzzled Jackson. He had not expected to run into this kind of trouble and the town's antagonism made him curious.

But it was more than an aloof hostility that he felt in Nick. There was a more personal emotion in the gunman's sneering regard. Naked in his eyes was the hot arrogance of a fast gunhand debating his chances with the known reputation of this big Ranger.

"I'll take the keys to that lock, Elias," Jackson said slowly. "I'm making my headquarters in this office."

Nick shook his head. "I've got my orders, Ranger. You heard Mr. Petersen tell me to lock this place up."

"Petersen own this building?"

"I wouldn't know." Nick's voice held a plain insolence.

Solitary considered this man's attitude. He had not come looking for trouble with any of Muleshoe's citizens. He remembered this and took a tight grip on his temper.

"I'll check on it," he decided. "I'll be around later for those keys."

A sneer spread across Nick's face. He was making this big Ranger back water and it put contempt in his voice.

"You may be a holy terror where you come from, Ranger. But to me you're just a big fella askin' for trouble. Don't crowd me!"

Jackson's anger showed briefly in his eyes. He knew Cates's kind. The man would keep after him now, made bold by Jackson's apparent hesitation to meet his challenge.

"I'll be back," he repeated bleakly. "Don't overplay your hand!" He turned the roan away before Nick could reply.

The gunman's laughter followed him, riding the first rise of wind off the desert, a moaning, gritty wind born somewhere over the burning reaches of the Escalante. A swirl of sand ran along the street and enveloped him; he felt the sting of sand against his neck.

The Ranger rode back to the Eldorado, his face dark, his emotion held tight by an iron will. He saw the men lined up along the front of the Oro Grande Saloon and he caught the run of contempt in their glances. Petersen was standing in the doorway of the *Chronicle*, a small smile on his face.

Nick's tone had been loud and the wind had carried it to them. Solitary saw this now and knew he had made a mistake.

He turned the roan to the hotel hitchrack and dismounted. There were half a dozen men on the hotel veranda. He could feel their expectancy, the quiet waiting. . . .

Solitary ducked under the peeled cottonwood pole and started up the steps. The sun shown red against the peeling clapboards, filtering through the piling dust clouds. It fell across the Ranger's boots, like spilled blood.

"I reckon Nick Cates figured you right," a cocky voice jabbed at him. "Six feet high an' yeller clear through!"

Jackson paused. His tight control crumbled and a soft sigh escaped from him as he turned to face the owner of the sneering voice.

He was standing by the veranda railing and men had given him quick clearance. Jackson looked him over, from flat-crowned black hat sitting at a cocky angle on a thatch of crisp red hair to dusty, hand-tooled boots. In between was a muscular body clothed in long black coat and black trousers. The coat was unbuttoned and a bone-handled Colt rode high, set for a left-handed cross-draw.

The flat-crowned hat and the red hair and the mock imitation of Doc Holliday in dress rang a bell in Jackson's head, and the name of this killer clicked into place.

Marvey Holt! One of the top guns in the recent San Saba range war!

Muleshoe was not the place he expected to find a gunslinger like Marvey Holt. But then this desert town was full of surprises. He checked the run of his thoughts and faced the sneering gunslinger, and the smile on his lips was small and humorless.

Marshal Benton seemed to have made no secret of having sent for him, and Muleshoe obviously had been waiting for him to show up. The town was waiting to see if Solitary Jackson measured up to his reputation; he was being judged and weighed. A cold and bitter anger glittered in the Ranger's eyes.

"You talking to me, son?"

Marvey grinned crookedly. "I hear you're the big bad Texas Ranger folks call Solitary Jackson. Heard about you on the San Saba, too. Some good friends of mine call you the bounty-hunting Ranger." He shook his head, slowly, making the gesture one of contempt. "From where I stand they got the story all wrong. Either you ain't this big bad Ranger, or you got a yeller streak in you a yard wide!"

A spinning puff of sand ran across the road and spilled between them. It hung for a moment like a flimsy curtain in front of Holt.

Jackson's voice tore through it, flat and wicked: "Seems like that Colt's too big for you, son. I'm going to take it away from you and ram it —"

Marvey slid into a crouch and his left hand stabbed for his gun.

The man in front of him seemed to vanish behind a burst of flame and a puff of black smoke. The bullet hammered the gun out of Holt's hand, glanced off, went through his coat and cut a three-inch gash across his right hip.

Weaponless, shocked into immobility, Holt stared at the big man. The Ranger dropped his Peacemaker into holster and backhanded Marvey across the mouth.

The blow spun the gunslinger against the railing. Pain and a blind anger jerked him around. He ran into an iron fist that doubled him; the hooking left hand, catching him squarely, dumped him over the railing. He landed on the back of his head and shoulders and didn't move.

It had ended so quickly some of the men crowding the hotel doorway had not seen it all.

Jackson scooped up Marvey's Colt, thrust it under his belt, and vaulted the railing. He came down beside the unconscious gunslinger, bent, came up with him across his shoulder.

The hotel crowd clustered on the stairs until they could determine where the big Ranger was headed. Then they followed, trailing at a cautious distance.

Jackson walked with a long stride toward Tom Benton's office. He went past the Butte View Lunchroom, and he saw Ruth Dillman and her father come to the door and stare after him. And then his attention was on Nick Cates, standing by the low adobe building, facing him.

Elias Woods had finished working on the lock. He had put his tools in his box and now stood staring at the burdened man coming toward them.

Jackson's voice reached out to the gunman; it rang flat in the street, rising above the wind. "I'll take those keys now, Nick!"

Nick Cates hunched his shoulders in momentary indecision. He had not clearly witnessed what had taken place on the porch of the Eldorado, and he didn't care if the man slung over the big Ranger's shoulder was dead or alive. But what he saw in this big man's eyes gave him a momentary surge of panic that ended in a cold, tight knot at the pit of his stomach.

"Don't crowd me, Ranger!" he snarled. "I told you to keep away —" He went for his gun in sudden decision.

Solitary's right hand disappeared in a burst of smoke. Nick spun around and fell against the adobe wall. He put out his left hand in a blind effort to hold himself erect. His nails left tiny marks on the wall as he fell. . . .

Solitary Jackson made a motion with his Colt. "Open the door," he told Woods. "Then hand me the keys."

The carpenter obeyed. He pushed the door open and held out the keys to the new lock.

Jackson took them as he walked inside with Marvey, who was beginning to stir on his shoulder. He walked the length of the dimly lighted room to the door in the rear which opened up to a back room with one smaller barred window and a cot against the wall. He dumped Holt on the straw mattress, closed and locked the door with the key still in the keyhole.

He paused by Tom Benton's desk, anger still bright in his eyes. Outside a crowd was gathering around the horse-faced gunman; he could hear their murmuring above the wind.

The sun was a pale red banner in the street and there was an irritating quality to the dust storm. Jackson took a deep breath. He had been pushed since his arrival here; there was an antagonism here he could not pin down.

There seemed to be an undercurrent of fear and distrust in Muleshoe, a bad combination to overcome. But with Benton no longer responsible, someone had to take over authority.

He walked to the door and faced the muttering crowd. "The name's Solitary Jackson," he announced flatly. "Texas Ranger. I'm the law here until you folks get yourselves another marshal!"

The crowd shuffled silently, accepting this with sullen acquiescence. Someone said, "We need more than a Ranger here —" but no one else took this up.

Jackson turned to Nick Cates who was trying to sit up; the man's lips were twisted in pain. He didn't look at the Ranger.

"Someone get him to a doctor," Jackson

ordered. "The rest of you go on home. There's not going to be any more trouble tonight!"

The crowd dispersed slowly, two of them helping Cates to his feet and taking him with them. Solitary let his attention turn to the darkening desert. The dust storm was at the edge of town now, and the wind had an ominous howl.

He turned to go back inside. Petersen's harsh voice stopped him.

"Just a minute, Jackson."

The Ranger turned to face the newspaper editor, a frown on his face. Petersen's head was bare; his eyes had an angry glitter. He shook a finger at Solitary.

"This won't get you anywhere, Ranger! Nick Cates was only obeying orders!"

"Your orders?" Jackson's voice was cold. He studied the man, trying to understand Petersen's hostility. Was it fear? Or did this man, so used to being the power in Muleshoe, hate to see someone else take authority?

"Did you order Nick to try to gun me?" he added softly.

"Of course not!" Petersen's face was flushed. "But I did tell him to lock this place up. You didn't have to prod him into a shooting over it."

Jackson's grin had a sour twist. "You got this thing turned around, Petersen. Your man did the prodding. And I don't take too much prodding!"

"I see." Petersen straightened, his back stiffening with outraged pride. He was a touchy man, Jackson saw, a man of quick anger and of long hate. A big man in a small town. Perhaps that explained Petersen's presence here on the edge of the desert, eight hundred miles from Texas authority. . . .

"I see," Petersen repeated. "Well, the governor will be in Muleshoe soon. I'll bring this matter of your highhandedness up with him." A grim smile lifted a corner of his thin-lipped mouth. "I think you know how he feels about the Rangers. When he hears how you are throwing your weight around —"

"Save it for Governor Coke!" Jackson interrupted harshly. "In the meantime, keep out of my way, Petersen!"

The *Chronicle* publisher flinched. A dark temper flared in his eyes; the lines bracketing his mouth deepened. He nodded, choosing his words slowly: "I will, Ranger. But just remember one thing. I didn't send for you. And as far as I'm concerned, you have no authority in Muleshoe!"

Deliberately, Jackson unpinned his badge from his wallet, pinned it to his shirt. He stood big in the doorway, a hard, unyielding man with the weight of Texas behind him.

"This is my authority, Petersen! Don't you ever forget it!"

Petersen sneered. He turned on his heels, his back ramrod stiff. The wind fluttered his coat about his thin shanks as he walked back along the dust-obscured street.

VI

Marvey Holt was sitting on the cell cot, holding his head in his hands, when the Ranger looked in on him. He lifted his gaze to the big man standing in the doorway. Jackson's right hand lay close to his Colt and a small, wry smile touched the San Saba gunman's lips.

"Feel hungry?" Jackson's voice was rough.

Holt shrugged. He touched his swelling jaw with the tips of his fingers. "Don't reckon I could eat right now anyhow," he muttered. "Got a headache, too. Damn it, Ranger, what did you hit me with — a club?"

Jackson ignored the rhetorical question. "Who hired you to brace me, Holt?"

Holt's eyebrows went up insolently. "So you know me, Ranger?"

"Nothing good," Jackson replied drily. "A young punk with a fast gun heading up the wrong trail on a fast horse. A kid who happened to be on the right side in the recent San Saba range war. Killed a tough gunslinger named Bill Langley and made a name for himself." Jackson nodded grimly. "You're not on our list yet, kid, but you're headed there fast!"

Holt leaned back against the wall. "No

sermon, Jackson. I'm not in the mood for it."

"I don't preach, kid." Jackson's voice was rough. He was a lone man in a tough town, and he didn't know what lay out there in the desert. He had no time for cocky gunslingers. "I just give orders!"

Holt's sneer was a little weak. "I'm listening," he muttered.

"I'm asking you once more. Who hired you to gun me?"

Marvey shook his head. "It was my own idea, Solitary. I wanted to find out if you were as tough as I had heard. When I saw you back down from that long-jawed gunman of Petersen's I thought you — Aw, hell!" He touched his jaw gingerly. "I found out what I wanted."

Jackson considered this. Holt could be a convincing liar.

"Look!" the young gunslinger said. "I just got into town a coupla hours before you did. Came in on the noon stage. You can check that. I don't know a soul in town. Nobody — nobody in town sent for me."

Jackson frowned. "All right, I'll believe that if you'll tell me why Marvey Holt comes four hundred miles to a small desert town. There's no range war going on here, kid. Nobody in town, except Petersen, who could hire a man like you —"

'This is a free country," Holt said bitterly. "Maybe I like it here. Might even have stopped off to look up an old friend —"

"Who?" Jackson's voice was sharp.

"I don't remember!" Holt heaved himself up and winced as his right leg sent a sharp pain through him. He put a hand down to his thigh and his fingers came away sticky with blood.

Jackson's voice was impatient. "You'll have a chance to sleep on it, Holt. I'll let you out of here in the morning. And I'll be with you when you buy a ticket on the morning stage out of here —"

"The hell I will!" Holt snarled. "I came here for a reason. I'm staying —"

"You'll go because I'm sending you!" Jackson's mouth was grim. "I've got enough troubles in this town without a gun-proddy fool like you out to try his luck!"

He started to leave, dropped his gaze to Holt's bloodstained thigh. "Reckon you'll need a doc to look at that?"

"No." Holt sat down again. "It's just a scratch. Leave me alone!"

Jackson shrugged. He closed and locked the door and turned to the office.

The sun had faded entirely in the interval he had been in the cell; the office was already gloomy. He had difficulty making out Tom Benton's pipe stand on the spur-scarred desk, the tin of tobacco, the old dodgers which were gathering dust. . . .

A tiredness weighed on the big Ranger as he stood there. He had come to Muleshoe to see Tom Benton, but the marshal had tried to kill him. The whole town was edgy, jumpy, and the antagonism he felt in Petersen was reflected in most of the faces he had seen. Why? What was he up against here?

Back in Austin there were rumors of the Baron and his desert empire. But the stories brought only amusement, a cynical tolerance. A harmless crank who wanted to take over eighty thousand square miles of desert from Texas.

But here the story was no joke. The threat out of the desert was real. It had Muleshoe scared.

Jackson touched the wiry bristle darkening his jaw and remembered that his roan was still at the Eldorado rail, and he shook his head at his forgetfulness.

The big stud snickered at his approach, turning to eye him with eager lift of head. Jackson ran a hand down the roan's flank. "Sorry, fella," he muttered. "I'll get you bedded down right away."

The dust storm cast a premature twilight over the desert town. The hotel veranda was empty of loungers. A sickly yellow light stained the dirty windows. The rising wind scattered sand across the plank walk.

Jackson pulled his neckerchief up to protect his face. Muleshoe had changed in the half-hour since he had walked from this building with Marvey Holt across his shoulder. It was a ghost town, boarded up against the oncoming sandstorm.

He mounted and swung away from the empty

rack. He headed east toward the end of Main Street. The small cemetery on the rise beyond was hidden by the swirling dust pall. The towering canyon walls that shut off the high range from the Llano Escalante loomed shapeless in the darkening night.

Jackson rode past the lighted windows of the *Chronicle* and was abreast of the sign before his slitted gaze made it out: *Amos Selwick, Livery Stable.*

He turned the roan under the wide board sign stretching across the alley and rode in darkness toward the acrid smell of manure and stable. He came out into a back yard with a big barn facing him, its door closed. He could barely make it out in the gloom.

He rode the roan up the wooden ramp and dismounted. The animal shifted impatiently, his iron-shod hoofs drumming on the scarred wood. Jackson put his shoulder to the door and it gave to his shove, rolling back on oiled overhead runners. The pale glow of a lantern spilled out, outlining the ramp.

Jackson led the roan inside. The wind swirled sand in after him and in the stillness it sounded like the quick scampering of mice.

Someone stirred in the darkness beyond the reach of the lantern. A man's sleepy voice muttered: "Be right with you."

Jackson pulled his neckerchief down from his face and spat grit from between his teeth. The hostler shuffled up into the circle of light and the

Ranger saw that his right arm was twisted and he carried it close in to his side. A rail-thin man with deep furrows in a worn face and a dull glaze in his bloodshot eyes.

Solitary knew the type. Probably a good enough cowhand until a riding accident had crippled him. Then years of drifting, looking for odd jobs, trying to hold on to a pride that had nothing tangible to uphold it.

He came to stand beside the roan; he ran his good hand along the big stud's flank.

"Nice cayuse," he mumbled. His breath smelled of cheap whisky and the stubble on his chin was at least five days old.

The roan turned and bared his teeth and the hostler grinned uncertainly. He took his hand away and glanced at Jackson. "One-man horse, eh?"

"Treat him gentle and he'll give you no trouble," Solitary answered. "He doesn't take to a rough hand."

"I'll treat him with kid gloves," the stableman answered. "Grain or hay?"

"Both," the Ranger replied. "And he'll stand a bucket of water."

He unsaddled the roan himself and watched the hostler lead him into an empty stall just beyond the reach of the lantern hanging from a nail on the wall. Other horses thumped uneasily. Jackson's idle thoughts settled on this small, shuffling figure thrust by bitter circumstance into eking out a living shoveling manure.

The hostler came back to join him. They stood within the small circle of light; the man leaned back against a loft support from which old harness hung. He was facing the open door where the wind was whirling sand like a circular curtain on the edge of the lantern light, shutting them off from the darkness of the yard.

"Helluva night," the stableman said. He fumbled in his bib overalls for a clay pipe. "Same kind of a night Bob Crane was killed."

Jackson was starting to roll a cigarette. He turned and looked sharply at the man, sensing something in his nervous tone.

"You knew Bob Crane?"

Judd Viers shrugged. "He used to come in here a lot," he said. "Liked to ride Nig over there." He pointed with his pipe stem to a dark shape in one of the far stalls. "Did a lot of riding for an Easterner. Claimed it was good for his health."

Jackson considered the unspoken message behind this man's conversation. Crane was the man who was killed by the odd arrow the night Marshal Tom Benton was shot. Had there been a connection?

"Reckon the riding caught up with him," Jackson observed. He cupped his match and brought it to his cigarette; his eyes had an alert, questioning glint as he looked at Judd.

The hostler licked his lips. He was studying this big Ranger covertly, as though trying to find his own courage in this tall, wide-shouldered figure with the silver star of Texas on his shirt.

He glanced out into the stormy night and rubbed his hand nervously across his stubbled jaw.

"I heard talk you're the Ranger Tom Benton sent for. The one they call Solitary —"

"I've been called that," Jackson admitted. He dropped his hands away from the cigarette, stepped on the wood match. "Why?"

"I'm just a bum," the hostler said. A pent-up bitterness broke through his caution. "Old Judd they call me. Old! Hell, I reckon I ain't a year older'n you!" He wiped his mouth again. "I sleep up in the loft with the rats, Ranger. I shovel manure an' water the hosses. I ain't nobody. But I see more than most people think — an' I hear a lot, too."

Jackson waited, knowing how it was with this man, knowing he had to let Judd talk his courage up.

"I got a pretty good idea why Bob Crane was killed, Ranger. I been keepin' it inside me. Ain't nobody in town I could talk to. Not with Tom Benton the way he is now —"

"Who was Bob Crane?" Jackson interrupted.

"Claimed he was an Easterner out here for his health," Judd repeated. "Mebbe he was. But he did a lot of ridin' for a sick man. An' they killed him the same night they got Benton —"

"They?" Jackson's voice lifted sharply.

"The Baron — or some of his bunch," Judd nodded. "Mebbe you can figure out what this means, Ranger." He reached in his patched overall pocket, fumbled around for something. "Picked this up outa the hay pile where Red Davis slept last night. Blind as a hoot owl, he was. Came in here to sleep it off. I saw him —"

He cursed as the small black notebook he pulled out of his pocket slipped through his nervous fingers. "Damn!"

Jackson bent swiftly to pick it up.

He heard the metallic twang from the darkness of the yard; something whistled ominously over his shoulder. He heard Judd gasp. . . .

He was crouched when it happened, and he reacted with instinctive speed. He lunged away from the doorway, reached the lantern. A quick puff plunged the barn into darkness. Then he whirled, faced the yard, a Peacemaker making its abrupt appearance in his hand.

He saw no one. The storm blanketed the shadows in the yard.

Judd's body was a dark, writhing shape a few feet from Jackson. His dying movements, blind and soundless, sent a chill through the big Ranger's spine. Finally a rattling sigh escaped the dying man's lips and his movements ceased. The stillness which followed seemed harshly acute, broken only by the low moaning of the wind outside and the run of sand particles across the stable flooring.

Solitary Jackson paced to the door opening and listened. Somewhere a door closed. But it could have been anywhere — and it might not have anything to do with the man who had killed Judd.

He could prowl through this town and find nothing; the futility of it brought a cold anger to his eyes. The killer was gone, vanished into the anonymity of this squalid settlement, cloaked by the howling desert storm.

He put his shoulder to the door and closed it. Then he turned and felt along the wall until he touched the lantern. The hot glass burned his fingers. He struck a match and touched it to the wick; the yellow light sent the shadows dancing over the far walls.

Judd lay huddled at the foot of the loft support, tangled in the harness. An arrow protruded six inches between his thin shoulder blades. It had entered his chest and gone all the way through his body. The stableman lay curled up like some small boy who had fallen asleep. His worn face was slack and vacant.

Jackson dragged the body over by the wall. He pulled the arrow out and draped a horse blanket over Judd. Then he examined the stubby, hardwood shaft.

It was almost an exact replica of the one Petersen had shown him. The same type of arrow that had killed Bob Crane.

There was a killer loose in Muleshoe, a maniac who used a strange bow. This was not an Apache arrow, nor was it Cheyenne. He had never seen an Indian arrow like it. And Jackson had seen many.

He shook his head. Why a bow? A rifle hit harder and reached farther. Perhaps the killer wanted to inject the element of fear, of the unknown, into his murders.

And why Judd? The broken-down hostler had indicated he knew something, but he had told Jackson little the Ranger had not already suspected. Why had the killer waited until this moment to kill the stableman? And then it occurred to Solitary that it may not have been Judd the killer had come after. He remembered that he had bent to pick up the notebook Judd had dropped the moment before the arrow hit the hostler. . . .

He blew out the lantern before opening the barn door and stepping into the yard. The wind buffeted him, filling his ears with sound. Jackson pulled his neckerchief up over his face again and jammed his hat brim down over his eyes. He ran across the yard to the partial shelter of the warehouse flanking the alley and turned to look back at the barn.

It loomed up dark and shapeless in the murky night, but Solitary had a sudden picture of the target he and Judd must have presented to the killer, standing, as they had been, in the lamplight. And to a man who knew how to handle a bow, twenty yards would present no problem, even on a night like this.

The killer was probably long gone, but some inner caution nagged at Jackson. He drew his Colt and held it against his side as he edged along the warehouse wall to the street.

The wind blew freely through the natural funnel of Main Street. The night seemed filled with a great soughing that smothered all other noise. Jackson forced his way against the buffeting storm, feeling his way back to the Eldorado.

He started up the steps, conscious of a sign somewhere creaking with nerve-rasping harshness. Then the sound of quick footsteps grating on the sandy plank walk behind him spun him around. His Colt muzzle leveled on the shadowy figure looming up.

The dark shape halted abruptly, warned by the cold glint of stray light reflecting from that ominous muzzle. A girl's near-hysterical voice asked: "Uncle Tom? Is that you?"

VII

Surprise pinned the Ranger to the wall. When he discovered it was a girl at the foot of the stairs he holstered his Colt and stepped down to join her.

A faint light from the hotel windows penetrated to the bottom of the steps and he caught a glimpse of Ruth Dillman's white face partially hidden by a yellow shawl. She recoiled as he loomed over her, and he put a hand on her arm.

His voice was sharp. "A bad night to be out, Miss Dillman. You in trouble?"

"No — no. I don't want to bother you —"

Jackson scowled. Just like the others in this town, he thought grimly. She seemed afraid of him, and strangely hostile. A rankling anger fretted him. He was not a lady's man, but he had never had trouble with women before. . . .

The wind moaned around the hotel corner; it buffeted them and made it quite uncomfortable to be standing there. Ruth pulled the shawl over her face and started to move away.

He stopped her. "What's the matter with you?" he asked roughly.

She looked up at him. "I — I thought you were Uncle Tom."

"Prowling around on a night like this?" His

tone held a heavy sarcasm.

She nodded, a bright anger in her eyes. "Yes. Prowling around, like you were just now, with a gun in your hand!"

"There's been some trouble," he said shortly. Then, "What's happened to Tom Benton?"

"He's gone." There was resentment in her voice. "Doctor Harrigan put him to bed. We left him in his room. Mother and I were in the house . . . we thought he was asleep —"

She shivered and panic crept into her voice. "I don't want him hurt, Mr. Jackson. And I don't want him hurting anyone. But he's out in this storm, and he's got his guns. I think he's out looking for you!"

Jackson sucked in a deep breath, filtering it between clenched teeth. For a brief instant he harbored a grim suspicion that Tom might have been the man who had killed Judd — but Tom was out with a gun, not a bow.

"When did you find out he was gone?"

"About twenty minutes ago. I was getting ready to come back and join Dad at the lunchroom — help out with the supper dishes. I took a look in Uncle Tom's room first —"

A gust of wind momentarily choked her; she gasped and tears came to her eyes.

Jackson took her arm. "We can't talk out here," he said flatly. "I'll take you home."

She shook her head. "Father's lunchroom," she gasped. Her voice was muffled behind her shawl. "It's nearer."

They crossed the street, fighting the wind. Jackson's wide shoulders crawled; the threat of a mad bowman and a crazy town marshal loose in this stormy night, both looking for him, brought a cold sweat to his face. He felt a quick relief when the lights of the Butte View Lunchroom appeared before them. He opened the door and followed Ruth inside.

The door closed out the storm, but not the threat of the night. Jackson walked to the windows and pulled down the shades and turned quickly as Sam Dillman snapped: "What in thunder are you doing that for, Ranger?"

"To save my hide," Jackson said calmly.

Sam glowered. He had been working over his books, hunched on a stool at the far end of the counter. There was no one else in the lunchroom.

He turned a worried face to his daughter as she went to him. "You didn't have to come back, Ruth. Business was light. I could have managed —"

"Uncle Tom's gone!"

The fear in her voice stopped him. He stared into her white face, down at her hands nervously fingering her shawl. Then he swiveled around to confront the big Ranger.

"You —"

"No, no! He didn't know —" Her voice rang tiredly in the empty eating house. She flung her shawl back on her shoulders and brushed sand from her eyelids. She slumped wearily on a stool.

"Uncle Tom took his guns with him. I think he's out there somewhere — looking for Mr. Jackson."

"You sure he's gone, Ruth?" Sam's voice was harsh. "Maybe he just went out to —"

"Mother and I looked everywhere," Ruth said. "He took his gunbelts and the rifle from your closet. He must have crawled out on the porch roof. We found the window open and the curtains blowing."

Sam shook his head. "Good Lord! Tom's in no condition to be out in that!" He turned to the Ranger. "Doc Harrigan bandaged that gash on his arm and told him to keep quiet for a few days. Told me later that Tom was suffering from pressure on the brain — some piece of bone he couldn't take out without risking Tom's life. But even so, he might drop any time —" He threw up his hands in disconsolate emphasis. "I can't account for Tom's actions when you showed up, Ranger. He had been waiting for you for months. Now — now he's probably trying to hunt you down and kill you!"

Solitary shrugged. "I think I can handle him," he said. He wasn't sure he could, but he felt he had to reassure these two people.

"You have any idea why he'd want to go out tonight?" he added. "Besides —" the Ranger's voice held a wry note — "wanting to kill me?"

Sam Dillman frowned. "Tom kept talking about something he had to get out of his office. Said it was from Bob Crane. I — I thought he was just talking. One day I even searched the place. I didn't find anything. He was with me, and I kept asking him what it was he wanted. But he just looked around with that vacant stare —" Sam bit his lips. He was a tired, worried man. "I didn't think he'd try a thing like this tonight."

"Well, I'll take a look around town for him," Jackson promised. "I'll check the office first. But he couldn't get in, anyway. It's locked." He knuckled his jaw thoughtfully. "Where else would he be liable to hang out?"

"The Oro Grande, sometimes," Sam said. "But Tom wasn't much of a drinking man. He liked to play checkers with Amos Selwick and George Vollmer at the stage office. George Vollmer is district manager for the Desert Line Company," Sam added.

Jackson remembered with a guilty start the dead man he had left behind in Selwick's stables. Amos was Judd's boss; he ought to know.

"Where can I find Selwick?"

"Same place," Sam answered, frowning. "Amos never misses a night. He's a bachelor —" He gave directions.

Solitary nodded. "I'll have to drop in on their game. I've got some bad news for Amos."

Sam closed his books and pushed them aside. "Ruth, get some coffee." He looked at Jim. "Bad news?"

Jackson told him about Judd Viers. "The same kind of arrow that killed Bob Crane," he said. "And I've just figured out the bow it came from." His eyes narrowed. "Been nagging at me since I saw the first one in Petersen's office. A crossbow —"

He smiled grimly at the incredulous look that spread across Sam's face. "I saw one once, in a museum in New Orleans — private collection, it was. I just happened to be along with a friend —"

"A crossbow?" Sam knuckled his forehead. "Ain't that an old type bow used in the Middle Ages?"

"Don't underestimate it, Sam," Jackson said. "It was good enough to penetrate armor." He shook his head. "I know it doesn't make sense. But it looks like someone's dug up a museum piece, or had a copy of one made, and is using it. My guess is that it's all part of a plan to scare hell out of people along the Escalante."

He had remembered the notebook Judd had dropped; he brought it out now. "Judd was going to show me this when he was killed. I haven't had a chance to look it over."

The notebook was old and dog-eared and held little more than half a dozen strange names and addresses, most of them from the East. They meant nothing to Jackson, nor to Sam, who looked at it over Solitary's shoulder.

Folded in between the pages, however, was an old, yellowed clipping. There was no dateline on it, nor did the clipping include the name of the paper from which it had evidently been taken. It read:

Surrounded by a score of witnesses, Clay Coke pistol-whipped Duncan Stafford today in a political argument which flared up over drinks in Clancy's Bar.

Bystanders testified that Duncan Stafford came into Clancy's looking for trouble. Coke was surrounded by half a dozen of his riders, but none of them took part in the quarrel which ensued.

According to eyewitnesses, Stafford called the big cattleman a liar and a crook and made further remarks concerning the dubious beginnings of the C-Bar-C Ranch. Stafford was quoted as saying: "I'll see you in hell before you're elected to Congress!"

The enmity between Stafford and Coke dates back several years to the time when the big cattleman pushed through a bill in the State legislature allowing him to build a dam on the . . .

The newspaper clipping was torn at this point. It was not a recent tear. Jackson pushed it over for Sam to read. He was frowning, pulling the fragments of this story into focus.

The Clay Coke mentioned in the clipping must be the present governor — Coke still owned the C-Bar-C Ranch on the Trinity. Coke had put in a two-year term as Congressman before that.

That would put the date of the clipping at least six years away.

But why did a man like Red Davis, an itinerant typesetter, have this clipping in his possession? Why was it important to him?

Sam Dillman turned a puzzled face to the big Ranger. "Doesn't mean anything to me," he said slowly. "Never heard of either of the two men in the story."

"You should have," Jackson said. "The Clay Coke in this story is Governor Coke. I understand he's due to come through Muleshoe on a political tour next week."

Sam pursed his lips. "You sure that's the same man?"

Jackson nodded. "Background's the same. Coke still owns the C-Bar-C on the Trinity —"

"What's this all about?" Ruth interrupted. She had come to the counter with coffee cups; she stood facing Jackson, and he noticed now that her eyes were a dark blue and held a softness in their depths. Her shawl was draped across her shoulders and she stood just below eye level. The lamplight touched up red-gold highlights in her hair.

"I'm not sure," the Ranger answered. "I don't know why Davis would be carrying a clipping like this, unless it was important to him." He folded it, tucked it between the notebook, and put it in his pocket.

"Judd thought it was important, too," he murmured. "Maybe it was just talk, Sam, but he was hinting that he knew why Bob Crane was killed. What did you know about Crane?"

The lunchroom owner shrugged. "Ruth knew him better than I." He turned to her.

"He was a gentleman," Ruth stated quietly. "He had a polite way of speaking, not only to women. He was a quiet sort of man. Wrote poems. Some of them were published in the *Chronicle.*"

"Judd said he did a lot of riding, mostly in the desert," Jackson commented.

"I — I think so. He asked me to go riding with him a few times. Said I was the only person in town —" she colored slightly — "who had read more than the local newspaper. He was always the gentleman. As he was from the East he told me of Philadelphia and Boston. Small talk, mostly. Only once did he speak of anything personal. He mentioned a younger brother. I gathered he was worried about him. He said they were different types, that he didn't like the way his brother was living. A fast gun and a yen for a fast dollar — that was the way he put it."

"Was that all he told you about his brother?"

"Yes. . . . Oh, he did say this." Ruth was frowning slightly, trying to remember Bob Crane's conversation. "He said that if anything happened to him, his brother would show up. Marvey was all the family he had, he said." She looked up at the big Ranger, her eyes glistening; there was a sadness in her voice. "He said to tell Marvey he was sorry. That's all. He said his brother would understand."

"Did his brother show up?"

Ruth shook her head. "No one's asked about Bob Crane since he was killed. We went through his personal belongings — he lived at the Eldorado — but there was nothing there to identify him. No letters even."

Marvey Holt? A fast gun admittedly in Muleshoe on his own. . . . Jackson took a deep breath. It could be. It could well be that the San Saba gunslinger was Bob Crane's brother.

He said: "Thanks for the coffee, Ruth. I'll take a look around for Tom. Don't worry about him. He's probably playing checkers with Amos and George, like you say he used to."

But as he stepped out into the howling night, the big Ranger wasn't so sure. . . .

Tom Benton stepped through the bedroom window onto the roof of the porch, ducked his head against the wind, and edged along the house side to the end of the roof. He leaned over the edge and dropped the rifle he carried onto the yucca Clara Dillman had planted against the side of the house; he jammed his Colts snugly into his shoulders and got down to his hands and knees.

He lowered himself slowly, seeking a handhold on the uncertain solidity of the gutter. The wind tugged at him, hurling a thousand tiny particles of grit into his face. He let himself hang by his hands and then dropped five feet to the ground.

The impact sent a pain jarring through his

head, and he set his teeth against it. He found the rifle he had dropped and tucked it under his left arm. The feel of it in his hands, added to the familiar weight of the guns at his hips, made him feel better than he had in days.

He was through with just sitting and waiting. The big man who claimed to be Solitary Jackson was just another phony, sent to kill him. Benton's lips curled. This time he'd do the hunting. . . .

But first there was something he had to find in his office. Something important. He didn't remember just what it was. But he did remember having hidden it in his tobacco tin. All evening the memory of it had nagged at him. Something important — something Bob Crane had given him.

He kept to the back yards and empty lots, fighting the howling wind, knowing by instinct which way to go. He left the protection of the last building to cross the road to the law office he had occupied for more than ten years.

He found the door locked. Benton had an old key with him, but the new lock did not respond to his efforts. A snarl twisted his lips. He stepped back a pace and fired three shots into it. The wind whipped away the reports, smothering them in its own savage fury.

He put his shoulder against the door and now it gave. He stumbled across the threshold.

The office was dark. But Tom Benton didn't need a light to find what he was after. He crossed to the desk and fumbled for the tobacco tin — he removed the cover and was digging inside when he heard the voice, muffled by the closed cell door.

"Hey, Ranger! Figured you had forgotten me!"

Benton stood still. Someone in the cell — someone who thought he was . . . He turned on his heel, taking the tobacco can with him, and walked to the door.

On the other side of that closed door Marvey Holt broke the stillness with brittle impatience. "Damn it, Ranger. I want to talk to you about my brother!"

Benton stood undecided. He was still holding the tobacco can in his hand, but he had forgotten why he had taken it. A strange trembling seized him. He dropped the can and put his hand on the door knob. But this room, too, was locked. He felt for the key which he always left in the lock when the cell was unoccupied, but it was gone.

Anger swept through the old lawman in an unreasoning burst of rage. He swung his rifle up and fired two shots at the lock. The slugs smashed off cast iron and whined into the cell. . . . He heard a man's sudden gasp of pain from the other side of the door.

Benton lifted his right foot and kicked the door in. He stepped across the threshold, his rifle muzzle threatening the figure doubled over against the wall.

Marvey was a darker bulk against the wall, but the old marshal's eyes made him out. The man's harsh breathing located him.

"Damn you, Jackson!" The prisoner's voice was thick with suppressed pain. "You didn't have to shoot your way —"

Jackson's name acted like a primer, touching off the blind pressure of hate in Benton. He caught Marvey by the shoulder, yanked him away from the wall, shoved him through the door into the office.

The younger man stumbled, fell against the door jamb, then fell forward to his hands and knees. Benton stood over him, breathing heavily. His head felt strangely light. It didn't pain him now.

"Who are you?" he demanded harshly. "What are you doing in here?"

Marvey tried to get up. One of Benton's rifle bullets had torn his side; it was not a serious wound, but it was painful and was bleeding badly.

"I'm Marvey Holt!" he muttered through clenched teeth. His vanity had taken a beating today; there was a grudging humbleness in his tone. "Bob Crane was my brother."

"Crane?" Benton touched his bandaged head. *Bob Crane? He had come here for something Crane had given him. Something important . . .*

He wheeled away from Marvey, found the lamp on the desk, lighted it. He turned, his features lined and harsh in the flickering light. He walked to the tobacco scattered over the floor and knelt to pick up a folded piece of paper.

Marvey Holt was staring at him. "Benton," he said wonderingly. "I thought you were that Ranger, Jackson!"

The ex-marshal whirled on him. "Jackson ain't here! I know! I sent for him. But he didn't come. They sent someone else — some killer who calls himself Jackson. They sent him to kill me! Because I know what's out there in the desert." His voice whipped up, wild and bitter. "Because I know how to find them!"

He waved the paper he had picked up at Marvey.

The San Saba gunslinger hitched himself to his feet. The man was crazy, he thought. That head wound of Tom Benton's was worse than anyone had figured.

"Give me a gun, Marshal," he said, thinking fast. He'd have to go along with Benton or wind up with a slug in his guts. "Give me a gun an' I'll help you get Jackson."

Benton's eyes narrowed. "You said you was Bob Crane's brother?"

Marvey nodded. The hand he was holding to his side was turning red. "I didn't want to disgrace Bob — took the name Holt. Came here because of a letter he sent me. He wrote he could use a fast gun —"

Benton nodded. He blew out the light and came back to Marvey. His voice was grim.

"If you're Bob Crane's brother we won't have

trouble. If you're not, you'll wish you were!"

The wind was blowing through the front door. The loose posters on Benton's desk had blown off; they swirled around the room like white fluttering ghosts.

"Get out!" Benton snarled. "I'll tell you where to go. Keep movin'. I'll be right behind you!"

VIII

Marvey stumbled out into the windstorm. He felt the presence of the rangy man behind him, and it was a spur, keeping him moving. He cursed with silent, bitter vehemence.

He had come to town expecting to find his brother, give him a helping hand and some insolent ready advice. He was a big man now. Marvey Holt, the kid who had gunned Bill Langley, tough Dakota gunslinger. . . .

He faltered and leaned against a dark wall and Benton's rough hand sent him staggering. The marshal's voice cut through the wind. "Back through this alley, fella!"

Marvey felt the town around him, but he saw little of it. The wind howled over the buildings like a sullen animal. Lamplight shredded against the flying sand. Doors were closed and many windows were shuttered. No one moved along the streets.

He kept his eyes slitted as he walked hunched slightly over to the side. His thigh felt stiff with pain; the blood had crusted over the cut from the Ranger's bullet. But the gash in his side still bled, and he began to feel light-headed. His mouth was parched.

He didn't know where he was headed. He wondered where the madman behind him was going. What did Tom Benton expect to do on a night like this?

They came into a yard through a hole in a sagging board fence and the strong ammonia odor told him he was near a stable. He heard the uneasy thumping of horses and now Benton took his arm, iron fingers closing over his wrist.

"Keep quiet. I'll do the talking. Old Judd knows me —"

They went up the wooden ramp. The door was open and their boots grated on the sand piling up inside.

Benton paused and let go of Marvey's arm. The gunslinger sagged against the protection of the inside wall. He couldn't see a thing. But a horse snorted somewhere in the darkness.

He saw vaguely that Benton had a gun in his left hand now; he was holding the rifle down by his right side. The ex-marshal had his back to him and for an instant Marvey Holt reacted to this opportunity. But he couldn't do it. He knew he didn't have the strength and his bitterness expressed itself in a futile groping along the wall, searching for some weapon. He found nothing.

Benton struck a match. The red glow held up close to his face gave his features a satanic cast. His eyes reflected the flame in miniature, as though that same fire was burning in Benton.

He found the lantern on the wall and lighted it. Then an inbred caution made him turn to the door, slide it shut.

Marvey noticed that though Benton's arm was bandaged he seemed able to use it. Probably doesn't even feel the pain tonight, he thought uneasily.

The body under the blanket attracted Benton. He squatted beside it, and drew the blanket back.

Judd Viers' face seemed yellower; some of the lines appeared to have faded in it, as though death was slowly erasing all traces of life.

Benton rocked on his heels. He looked down at the man, making no comment, seeming to ignore Marvey. The San Saba gunman began to slide along the wall. He needed the support. His legs were rubbery. His eyes were on the pitchfork leaning against the near stall boards, just on the edge of the lantern light.

If he could reach it before Benton roused himself . . .

The ex-marshal remained hunkered on his heels, as though he had forgotten the Colt in his hand and what he had come for. Then his eyes focused on the arrow lying beside Judd's body. He picked it up and in a fit of anger he broke it in two and tossed it away.

Marvey was a yard away from the pitchfork when Benton got to his feet. He turned slowly and looked at Marvey. He seemed to be staring at something behind the gunman, searching the long-far distances.

Then his Colt came up, slowly, until the ugly

black muzzle centered on Marvey's stomach. Holt's muscles tightened and he felt a sour burning taste in his throat.

He waited, not daring to move a muscle. The silence spread between them and became a void in which the uneasy movements of the horses seemed far away. His muscles began to ache and sweat came out over his body and glistened on his face.

Benton smiled. Then he began to chuckle. He walked toward Marvey, his gun still centered on Marvey's stomach, his laughter growing wilder with each step.

Then he stopped. Abruptly. His eyes moved swiftly over the stable, as though he had suddenly come back from some far away place.

"We'll ride," he said. "I'll saddle Nig, that big black over there. Nice cayuse. Your brother used to ride him. . . ."

Marvey's breath expelled in a low whistle of relief. His lips tightened. "Ride? In that storm? You're cr—" He caught himself, biting down on his tongue. He had to watch himself with this man. One wrong word and that muzzle would explode into flame. . . .

"We'll ride!" Benton repeated harshly. "You are Bob's brother, you say? Then you'll want to find those who killed him. I'll show them to you!"

He went into the black's stall and led him out. There were saddles on sawhorses. While Marvey watched, too spent even to think of the pitchfork now, Benton saddled the big black and thrust his rifle into the scabbard.

Jackson's roan was in the next stall. He moved up close, but the roan bared its teeth. Benton stopped. He shook his head. "Nice animal, but too much trouble to break. Probably be fighting us all the way."

He picked out a spotted gray mare, saddled her. Then he led the animal to Marvey, jammed his Colt against Holt's side.

"You'll ride, huh?"

Marvey climbed into saddle, assisted by the former marshal. He waited, sagging over the horn. Benton walked to the door, pushed it far back on its overhead runners. Then he walked to Nig and swung into saddle.

"Let's go!"

Marvey ducked as they rode through the doorway. Shod hoofs pounded briefly on the ramp. He felt the tiny burning needles of sand begin to cut his face.

He was too tired and too weak to even curse the man who loomed up at his side and took the reins from him.

The big Ranger was half an hour too late. He found the door open. Sand gritted underfoot as he stepped inside the marshal's office. He lighted a wood match and found the lamp. The chimney was still warm to his touch.

The bullet-splintered doors told him what had happened. But the bloody handprint on the cell door frame puzzled him, as did the smudged prints on the gritty floor.

Tom Benton had obviously taken Marvey Holt with him. But why? And why had he shot the San Saba gunslinger?

Tobacco was scattered about the cell door and the almost empty can glinted from a corner of the room. But the pipe stand on the desk held its full quota of pipes.

Jackson tried to puzzle out Benton's moves, but none of them made sense. According to Sam Dillman, the marshal conceivably had come back to his law office for something. But Benton could not have known about Marvey Holt, nor could Solitary imagine what Benton wanted with the prisoner.

He blew out the light and went to the door. Tom Benton had not returned to the Dillman house. Then where had he gone? It was no night to be traveling. And yet . . .

Jackson had a sudden hunch that Benton had left town and had taken Marvey Holt with him.

He bucked the storm back to Selwick's stables and knew he had guessed right. The door was wide open, and the lantern, which he had put out, was burning brightly.

Jackson drew his Colt as he went up the ramp.

There was no one inside. Only Judd — and Jackson saw that the blanket over the body had been pulled back, exposing the hostler's face. He found the two pieces of the arrow against the back wall.

Further searching revealed that the big black stallion Judd had called Nig was gone. He could not tell what other animal had been taken, but it was logical to assume that Tom Benton would not be riding double on a night like this.

The roan nickered as he passed his stall and Jackson paused to pat the sleek hide. "Glad he didn't try to take you, fella!"

He had few friends and no family, and this animal was as close to him as anything else on this earth.

The roan tried to muzzle him over the boards. He pushed the wet muzzle away, grinning. He walked back to the lantern, blew out the flame. He stood in the darkness, hating to go out again in that bitter dust storm. But he had one more chore to do tonight. . . .

IX

George Vollmer chewed on the stump of his fat cigar and eyed the checkerboard with morose distaste. He was in the process of losing his fifth game to the fat man across the table, but it was not this which made him irritable. He could afford the fifty-cents-a-game stakes.

Outside the office the wind rampaged. Sand filtered in through the crevices and under the sills. The lamp flame flickered and danced as if caught in the night's wildness.

Amos Selwick stroked his gray-shot chin whiskers. He had a business which paid him a living, and a natural disposition for physical inactivity. He was fat-soft in a land of wire-hard men, but this did not bother him.

He said, with the bare hint of impatience: "You've got three moves left, George —"

The hammering on the door made him jump. He turned to face the front windows and apprehension made its brief glitter in his soft brown eyes.

George scraped back his chair and stood up. He was a short man with a solid, hard-muscled body, a sharp military mustache, ruddy cheeks. His brown suit fitted rather snugly across his thick shoulders. He was thirty-five, only a few years younger than Amos, but he looked a good deal younger and much more fit.

He took a Smith and Wesson revolver from his desk drawer and walked to the bolted front door.

"Who is it?" he growled.

"Jackson! Texas Ranger!" The voice came through the door panels, hard and clear.

George stiffened. Panic appeared in his hard gray eyes. Then he forced a frown across his face and slid the bolt back. He pulled the door open and stepped back, his pistol held at his side.

"Come in, Ranger," he invited gruffly. "Helluva night to be out calling, though."

Solitary moved into the office, a big, wide-shouldered man with a neckerchief pulled up across the bridge of his nose. His yellow-flecked eyes made their quick survey of the stage office as he pulled the bandana down. He took off his hat and slammed it against his knee, dusting it.

George slammed the door shut and put his back against it and studied Jackson with little friendliness. He saw the Ranger turn and glance at his gun and he made a short, disparaging gesture.

"Didn't know who might be out there, Ranger," he explained. "After what's been happening in town a man gets cautious about sticking his head out at night."

Jackson nodded. He turned his attention to the fat man at the table. "You Amos Selwick?"

The livery owner nodded.

The stage line manager shoved his pistol back in his desk drawer and took a clean glass out of another drawer. He introduced himself. "I'm George Vollmer. Join us in a drink, Ranger?"

"The name's Jackson," Solitary reminded. His voice was blunt. "I'll stay for the drink — and some information."

Vollmer rolled his cigar between his lips. His hand shook a little as he poured from the bottle on the table by the checkerboard.

"We were talking about you, Jackson. A lot of us feel we need a man like you in town." He held out the whisky glass. "Too bad you had that run-in with Tom Benton. And with that gunslinger who checked in at the Eldorado today."

"You forget Nick Cates," Jackson said coldly, accepting the glass.

"Cates got what he had coming to him, far as I'm concerned," Amos chipped in. "I'm sorry about Tom though. He was a damn good town marshal until that bullet put him on queer street —"

George Vollmer filled in at Amos' pause. "Well, looks like you've taken over, Ranger. Got things pretty well under control in town now —"

"Sorry to disillusion you," Jackson countered thinly. "Things are way out of hand." He turned to Amos who was eyeing him with slack-jawed interest. "I've got bad news for you, Amos. Judd's dead."

Amos blinked. He stared at the big Ranger,

then blew noisily and sagged back in his chair. "Judd?"

"Someone put an arrow through him, less than an hour ago," Jackson said. "He was talking to me when it happened."

"Why?" Amos shifted his heavy bulk in his chair. "Damn it, Ranger, *why?* Judd was a busted-up bum. Didn't own anything and never harmed anyone —"

"Maybe he knew something of what's going on around here," Jackson answered evenly. "And maybe the arrow wasn't really meant for him." He went on to tell them what had happened at Amos' stables.

"I left Judd there," he concluded. "Covered with a blanket. No way to leave a man, though. I thought you ought to know, Amos. If he had any next of kin —"

Amos shook his head. He looked shocked. "I'm about the only friend Judd had."

Jackson finished his drink and put the glass down on the table. "I've run into trouble since I arrived in town," he said bluntly. "I haven't had a chance to catch up. Maybe one of you can fill me in on what's been happening around here. What's got this town scared?"

Vollmer didn't meet the big Ranger's probing glance. He poured himself another drink.

Amos said, "Ain't any secret, Ranger. There's a bunch of killers on the loose — renegade whites and some Apaches off the San Juan Reservation. They raid out of the desert and disappear into it. A crazy fool who calls himself the Baron heads the bunch." He pushed his half empty glass aside. "Killed Judd, eh?" His voice had a sag to it. He turned to the stage line manager: "By thunder, George, I've about had enough. If I can find a fool willing to buy my business, I'm clearing out!"

Vollmer took his cigar stub from his mouth and spat shreds of tobacco on the floor. He gestured to a squat iron box in a corner of the office.

"If I don't get that money out of here soon, I'll be out of a job. I've got twenty-five thousand dollars in bullion in there, Jackson. Got to ship it to Harrisburg by the tenth. But I can't find a driver willing to risk it, nor a man with guts enough to ride shotgun —"

Jackson frowned. "Why not?"

Vollmer flung up a thick arm in an impatient gesture. "They're afraid of the Escalante raiders. Of this hombre who's been tacking up posters all along this end of the Llano. The Baron."

"Any idea who this madman is?"

George shrugged. "Don't think anyone around here knows that, Jackson. But whoever he is, the law can't seem to touch him. Sheriff Crowley took a posse out after them the day the Escalante bunch held up and robbed the Daylight Special just outside Concho. Went into the desert after them. Crowley had twenty armed men with him. They got lost in the breaks past Iron Butte —" Vollmer lifted his shoulders. "Less than twelve men got back to town with whole hides. Crowley was one of them. He hasn't gone into the Escalante since."

Amos was staring vacantly at the checkerboard. "They've got a hideout in the Escalante," he muttered. "They raid like Apaches and kill like Apaches. And no one's been able to track them to wherever they hang out. Storms keep wiping out tracks —"

Jackson was remembering the way Judd had died. No doubt the raiders did have a hideout in the desert. But one of them, the crossbow killer, hung out in Dry Gulch. It had to be that way.

He started to leave when an idea checked him. He turned to face George Vollmer.

"You say you have twenty-five thousand dollars you've got to ship to Harrisburg by next week?"

George nodded.

"Find me a driver," Jim said. Little cold lights were dancing in his eyes. "I'll see that the shipment gets there."

Vollmer's mouth opened. His cigar fell to the floor. "You?" he whispered. "When?"

"The sooner the better," the big Ranger replied.

George shook his head. "I don't think I'll find anyone willing to try it. Even for double wages and with you riding shotgun!"

"Pass the word around town!" Jackson ordered flatly. "And don't try to hide the fact that you'll be shipping the bullion!"

Vollmer's eyes had a muddy tinge. "I can't do it, Ranger, unless you sign a statement making you personally responsible for that shipment."

Jackson nodded. "I'll be responsible." His voice was bleak. "Just get me a driver!"

Amos stirred after the Ranger had departed. He shook his head. "You believe him, George? You think he's fool enough —"

"I quit believing in fairy stories," George cut in. His voice was angry. "Tom Benton sent for him, Amos. Tom swore by him. If you listened to Tom this Ranger was a combination of Wild Bill Hickok and —"

He threw up his hands and started to pace the office. Amos stared down at the checkerboard. "Judd," he muttered. "Never harmed anybody —"

He pushed his pieces into the center of the board and got up. "I've had enough for tonight, George. I think I'll go home. . . ."

George stared at the checkerboard a long time after Amos left. He, too, was a bachelor and lived in quarters back of the office. He was an ambitious man. There was a time when he had been a junior partner in a big wagon outfit in St. Louis. There had been a girl . . .

But he had wanted to get ahead too fast. He hadn't been content with being a junior partner. He wanted to own both the wagon outfit and the girl — and he lost both.

His name wasn't George Vollmer. Under his

real name he was wanted in the state of Missouri for murder.

He walked over to the window and stared at his own dim reflection in it. He had come to a dead end in this hot stinking corner of Texas, but there was no place else he could run.

After a while he blew out the light and went into the back room which served as sleeping and living quarters for him. It was neatly furnished, it had taste, and the books stacked in the small walnut bookcase were those read by an educated man. Usually he read himself to sleep, on the nights Amos left early, but tonight he was uneasy.

The knock on the bedroom door startled him, although he had been half expecting it. Still, he went back into the darkened office for his pistol; he was holding it as he unlocked the door.

The caller came in with a rush of wind; he closed the door and leaned against it, a shapeless figure in the darkness of the room. Vollmer turned to the lamp on the small stand by the bed, but the man's sharp voice halted him.

"No lights tonight, George."

Vollmer paused.

"He was here tonight?"

"Just left," George replied. "A few minutes before Amos."

The figure was silent, unmoving. Then his voice broke the uneasy stillness. "Missed him tonight. Must have some guardian imp standing watch over his hide, George. I had him lined up;

he ducked just in time."

"You killed Judd," George said. His voice held a remote distaste.

The shadowy figure shrugged. There was another pause. "What did he want here?"

"Guess he wanted to see Amos about Judd." George sounded tired, and afraid. "He's dangerous. He's not just another lawman — not like Tom Benton or that Federal detective, Bob Crane. And he's not the kind of fool Sheriff Crowley —"

"I know, I know," the caller snapped.

George's voice took on a nervous edge. "Then do something! If you let him nose around too long —"

"I can always bring Jode Slade into town," the other said. "Two or three of the others."

"Slade's not good enough!" George stated emphatically.

The shadowy visitor chuckled. "Don't ever let Jode hear you say that. Ever since he heard Tom had sent for Jackson he's been waiting for a chance to match guns with him."

George shrugged. "Then let him." There was a sneer in his voice. "I don't like Jode, anyway. He's getting big in that saddle, Baron. Some day he'll reach out and take over —"

"It worries you, George?"

The stage line manager sat on the bed. "Not too much, if you must know. I'm ready to move. But I thought you —"

"After next week I don't care if Jode takes

over," the caller said cryptically. His chuckle sounded again. "In fact, I'll make it easy for him, George. He's welcome to it."

"All your work," George protested. "It's beginning to pay off. Amos said tonight he'd sell for a song to clear out. Most of the ranchers along the Llano are moving out —"

"Jode's welcome to all of it," the other said. He was silent for a while, chuckling softly. "Let the wrath of the Lord — or more aptly, the wrath of Texas — fall on him."

George shifted uncomfortably. "The wrath of Texas is a long way off," he muttered finally. "Jackson is our only problem right now."

"We'll get rid of him. Before next week." The caller moved into the room. "It's got to be before next week, George!"

"Wait!" George was frowning. "Jackson's got something up his own sleeve. He wants me to get him a driver. He wants to ride shotgun on that bullion shipment I've got locked up in the safe."

"When?"

"Tomorrow. As soon as possible, he said."

"Good." The shadowy figure chuckled. "We'll get him a driver — and an escort, too." His voice held a thin excitement. "You'll do the driving, George. When you reach the fork this side of Iron Butte, take the short cut through Dawson's Gulch, up by those old abandoned mine shafts —"

"Wait a minute!" George snapped. "Why me? I don't like the idea of sitting next to that Ranger when he finds out."

"He won't have a chance to lay a finger on his Colts," the man promised. "But if it'll make it a little easier to take, there's twenty-five thousand in it for you!"

George's breath sucked in sharply. "The bullion?"

"It's yours," the other said. "Jackson will disappear with the stage. You come back with a story. Who's going to call you a liar?"

George absorbed this in the momentary silence which followed. This was the chance he had been waiting for since he had holed up in the squalid desert town. A big enough stake to take him to Mexico, completely removed from the threat of the law in Missouri.

"Besides," the voice continued, "who'll be worrying about a small thing like twenty-five thousand dollars after what's going to happen next week?"

George shook his head. "I don't get you. What will happen next week?"

The caller began to laugh. There was madness in it, an off-key timber. It made George shiver.

"The biggest shock to hit Texas since the Alamo, George." The man's laughter died, trickling into the silence of that room.

"And Jode Slade will inherit the consequences," he added coldly. "Jode Slade. . . ."

X

The dust storm was a wild thing attacking them. Marvey Holt kept his head down and his eyes closed; his bandana was pressed over the bridge of his nose and shielded his mouth. Even so, grit got between his teeth and dried his mouth.

The pain in his side receded, came again with burning insistence, receded once more. He tried to favor his side, and his muscles grew numb from the unequal burden placed on them. His mind seemed to grow numb, too.

He could feel Tom Benton's shadowy bulk riding up ahead, and once, rousing himself, he felt the edge of fear run cold fingers down his spine. If Tom ever let go the reins of his animal he'd be lost in this howling dark world of blowing sand.

Time faded into eternity. After a long, long time panic crept into Marvey Holt. He began to wonder if this crazy man knew where he was going. Or was Tom Benton lost?

Some time during that nightmare ride the winds began to subside. Marvey opened his eyes to find himself riding down a slope. It was still dark, but there was a grayness to the arching sky and only a few stars showed.

They reached the bottom of the slope and entered a canyon that brought night back again, blotting out the dim gray world. He closed his eyes, thankful that at least the storm had rolled past them.

When he opened his eyes again he saw the shack, a dark bulk against a shadowy wall. Somewhere off in the darkness he could hear the unmistakable murmur of water dripping over rock. . . .

A brush-topped ramada flanked the shack. Tom Benton rode up to it and dismounted, dropping the reins of Holt's animal. He led his black under the shelter and turned to Holt.

"Get down, Holt. I'll take a look at that cut on your side for you. . . ."

Marvey stood limp in saddle, feeling surprise crawl sluggishly through him. Benton sounded almost rational.

"Come on. Let's get inside." Benton's voice was impatient.

Holt gritted his teeth. His leg felt like solid lead as he lifted it over the saddle horn. He stepped down and staggered dizzily; he felt weak as a kitten and for the first time in his life he felt humility.

He had always been arrogantly sure of himself, confident in his physical strength, unbeatable with the gun strapped low on his hip. His arrogance had increased after the San Saba affair. He had come riding into Muleshoe, a cocky youngster condescending to help his brother.

But this confidence had been rudely knocked out of him today. First by an iron-fisted Ranger, and now by a grizzled town marshal to whom his reputation meant little.

Humility was a new emotion for Holt and he didn't like it. He pushed away from his horse and turned to the shack; he took three faltering steps before pitching forward on his face.

Tom Benton picked him up and carried him into the shack. Pack rats scurried away across the sandy floor, making little squeaks of alarm in the dark. Tom Benton knew this cabin, for he found the wooden bunk against the wall and laid Holt down on it.

The wind was still in the canyon. After the long hours of the night the silence now seemed to press like cotton wadding against Holt's ears. He heard the grizzled lawman move about in the dark, then a match flared and a moment later the flare strengthened, shouldering away the shadows.

Marvey turned on his side on the lumpy straw mattress and watched Tom bring the stubby candle over and set it on a wooden box next to the bunk. The marshal's tall shadow kept sliding in and out of the open door.

Holt gritted his teeth and tried to sit up. His head was spinning.

Benton stood over him, frowning. The bandages around his head were a dusty gray, his face was stubbled and gaunt, but his eyes had a look of concern in them.

"Hurt bad, kid?"

Marvey put his palm to his side, shook his head. "Lost some blood, that's all."

Benton grinned sourly. "I'll get some water."

He went out and Holt looked around, hoping to find some weapon left behind by a former occupant. But the cabin was Spartan in its bareness. This hard, board-framed bunk, the wooden box on which the candle sat, another crate nailed to the opposite wall to serve as cupboard, a small, rusted Franklin stove with a chunk of rock in place of a missing leg. The candlelight didn't quite light up all the corners, but Holt saw enough to discourage him.

Some lonely prospector's shack, long abandoned. He took a slow breath and lay back against the tinder-dry boards and tried to think. . . .

The marshal came back within a few minutes. He loomed up in the candlelight, looking taller than he was, and iron hard. He had a bucket of water which was leaking badly through its dried-out joints. He set it down by the bunk and Holt, licking his paper-dry lips, said, "I'm dying of thirst, Benton."

The marshal shrugged and lifted the bucket into Holt's hands. The San Saba gunslinger buried his face in the water. It had an alkaline taste, but it felt cool to his lips and he drank thirstily. After a while he set it down at his feet and looked up at Tom Benton.

The marshal said, "I'll have a look at that cut now, kid."

He helped Holt peel off his shirt and pull his trousers down from the bullet tear. Holt's underwear had absorbed a lot of the bleeding; it was stuck to the cut.

Benton eyed it doubtfully. "Gotta get a clean bandage over it or it'll get infected, kid. You game?"

Holt set his teeth. "Go ahead."

Benton squatted beside Holt. He cupped some of the water and sprinkled it over the blood-soaked area. After a while he used his knife and cut around the wound. Then he took one end of the wool patch which remained and tugged gently.

Holt winced and a thin gasp escaped his lips. The pain was like a knife reaching under his ribs.

Benton grinned. "It's gonna hurt a little more, kid —" and yanked roughly.

The pain exploded in Holt's head. He twisted violently, his eyes rolled and the breath went out of him. He was relaxed now in a place beyond immediate pain.

Tom Benton looked at the bright blood beginning to flow from the cut. . . .

Holt opened his eyes. He stared up at the cobwebbed ceiling for a long dull moment before he realized that it had lightened appreciably in the shack. The thought that he must have been unconscious for quite a while pushed through the thickness of his mind.

He sat up and felt the bandage at his side tug at him. He swung his legs over the bunk and examined the bandages. Tom Benton had done a good job with strips from somebody's old shirt. The rest of it was still on the box by the candle, which had been snuffed out.

Holt's lips twitched.

There was a small, flat bottle with about an inch of what looked like whisky in it on the floor by the box. It had not been there when Benton had brought him to the bunk, he was sure of that.

He looked around the shack. Benton was gone. A sick feeling knotted his insides. Benton was unpredictable. He might have gone and left him here, taking both horses.

Holt got to his feet. His legs felt rubbery and a cold sweat broke out across his back. He fought the weakness that started his head spinning, and when the room steadied he walked to the door.

The first thing he saw were the two horses, dozing in the shelter of the ramada.

Relief flooded him. He leaned weakly against the door frame, feeling the stiffness in his side and his thigh. Benton was nowhere in sight. The wind had died down altogether, and it was nearly morning. Somewhere a bird whistled cheerily.

Hope crept back into Marvey Holt. He was weak, and he didn't have an idea in the world where he was. But out there was a horse, and if he could get aboard he could leave this crazy marshal.

He took a deep breath and started for the ramada.

The gray mare he had ridden here woke. She turned her head and looked at him through big soft eyes. Holt reached the weathered pole support and clutched at it, feeling very tired. His muscles quivered. He took a look around again, wondering where Benton had gone to.

The canyon continued around the projection of limestone beyond the shack. He could still hear the quiet tinkle of water from that direction. Benton was probably at the spring. Holt turned and put his attention on the two saddles against the cliff which made up the ramada's rear wall.

Benton's rifle was still in the scabbard of his saddle.

Holt moved slowly around the pole and moved in between the two animals to the saddles. He bent slowly and got his hands on the stock and started to slide it free.

Benton's voice had an odd quality, thin and suspicious. "You got no need for that, kid —"

Holt stood crouched, not daring to move. His side began to ache. But he didn't move. The odd note in Benton's voice, the thin edge of uncertainty, brought sweat to Holt's face. It was as though the man behind him was doubtful of his own intentions, as though Benton was balanced on the knife edge of murder. . . .

The silence dragged and Holt's back felt exposed and painfully sensitive. He licked his lips, forced a mutter between his teeth: "I thought you'd gone an' left me, Marshal."

There was no sound from behind him. The horses moved uneasily, as though they felt the strain in the air.

Holt's side was beginning to cramp. He couldn't stand the tension any longer, so he straightened slowly and turned, lifting his arms away from his sides to show that he was unarmed.

Along the rim of the eastern wall the sky was bright. The stars were gone. He dropped his gaze to Benton, standing a few paces away. The marshal was holding a Colt in his hand, but he seemed to be looking past Holt, looking again into the far distances that seemed to have a peculiar meaning for him.

The gunslinger's gaze moved down to Benton's feet. There was a small, open-topped wooden box nudging the marshal's toes. The round, pale yellow cylinders nestled in sawdust didn't need the painted information on the box to tell Holt what they were.

Dynamite!

Slowly Benton lifted a hand across his face. He seemed to shake as though under a cold wind, then his eyes became attentive and focused on Holt. A slight grin cracked his hard lips.

"Glad to see you up and moving around, kid. Now get back in the shack. Catch up on some sleep. We'll be riding tonight."

Holt obeyed. He had to. Between his off moments, Tom Benton was rational enough to give the impression he knew what he was doing.

He walked back to the cot and sat down. Benton came inside and placed the box of dynamite in a corner and pointed to several unlabeled, rust-spotted cans on the box which served as table.

"We'll have to take potluck, kid. My guess is they're beans. Abe was sure gone on them."

"Abe?"

"Yeah — Abe Slater. Old coot who used to live out here whenever he could find somebody to grubstake him. He and I were the only ones who know about this place, I reckon." Tom walked over to the box and picked up the bottle of whisky. "Found this and a couple of clean shirts in the shaft by the spring. And these cans —"

"Where's Slater?" Holt was making conversation, studying Benton. The man seemed rational and sure of himself.

"Abe's dead. Old age snuck up on him while he slept. Right in that bunk —" He grinned as Holt involuntarily straightened.

"Young feller like you doesn't think of dying that way, eh?" He chuckled. "Maybe you won't, at that. Maybe you'll die like your brother —"

Holt's eyes narrowed. "You knew about Bob?"

Benton shrugged. "No. He worked on his own, it seems. Until the night he was killed —"

He reached in his pocket and took out a knife. "Ever see this before?"

Holt shook his head.

"This was your brother's."

"I haven't seen my brother in five years," Holt said. Then he remembered that Bob was dead and he would never see him again. His voice was bleak. "Last time I saw him I laughed at him. Told him he was a fool. He was working for a hundred a month as a Federal dick. I was gonna make my pile the easier way."

"Federal detective?"

"Yeah," Marvey muttered. "Bob worked for the Post Office. He was in Muleshoe investigating the mail robbery aboard the Daylight Special that took place just outside of Concho."

Benton ran a forefinger under his nose. "He did a good job, kid. I didn't know — He had us all fooled. Until the night he was killed, anyway."

"I came here to help him," Holt said bitterly. "I was feeling pretty cocky, Marshal. I got a reputation up around San Saba way. I was gonna ride in and give Bob a hand, show him how I handle things. . . ."

Benton jammed the knife blade into the top of the nearest can. He began to work the blade around the top.

"You still can, kid. Bob was killed because he found out where the Baron and his bunch hide out. He must have known they were after him the night he was killed. He told me how to find that hideout."

"You talked with Bob?"

"No." Benton fished in his pocket and tossed a folded slip of paper to Holt. "That was tied to your brother's knife. He tossed it into my office before he was killed."

Holt spread the note out and read it. He read it twice before he raised puzzled eyes to Benton.

"This? Sounds like some of Bob's poetry."

Benton snorted softly. "I thought so, too, at first. Then I remembered something. Old Abe Slater used to be a seaman in his younger days. Sailed aboard whalers for six years. When he came out here he had a binnacle light with him. He set it up on the cliff up here, right after he built this shack. Claimed it showed him the way home when he left Muleshoe two sheets to the weather."

Holt licked his lips and read the note again. "This is east of Muleshoe then?"

Benton nodded. "Tonight we go west, kid. We go west until we see a rock that looks like a skull."

"And then?"

"Then we'll wait." A hardness crept into Benton's voice. "We'll wait until they ride again, Holt. And when they do we'll follow them to their roost. . . ."

XI

Just before dawn that same day a rider dismounted on the shoulder of the Iron Butte and climbed the rest of the way up the steep face to a promontory facing the badlands. He had made this trip before, and always for the same purpose. He found the big mirror in the rock cache and waited for the sun to rise a little above the far misty rim of the desert, smoking a cigarette with stolid patience.

He was a short, thick man, native to this land of sun and distance. A mixture of Mexican, Indian and Irish, he had been formed and molded in the heat of the border sun.

Finally he ground his second butt under his heel. The mirror in his hand sent its flash of light across the gullied, desolate stretch of the Escalante — a long flash, then two quick ones. He repeated this several times. Then he replaced the mirror, smoked another cigarette. He was in no hurry as he climbed down to his waiting horse.

He figured it would take Jode Slade and the others a good three hours to get here. . . .

At eight-thirty that morning Ruth Dillman came to the door of her father's lunchroom. The morning rush had ebbed and she wanted a breath of air while it was still cool. She had slept little last night and the strain of worry showed in her face; it was paler than usual and the spray of freckles across her pug nose stood out in sharp contrast.

Ruth had lived in Muleshoe since she had come here, a girl of ten — the year before her brother died. The brown and ugly hills surrounding this desert town had grown into her very life and she seldom noticed them. But now she was looking at them, wondering if they held her uncle's body in some stony gully.

There had always been a certain amount of violence in this mining town. She had grown up with it. But only in the past year had terror cast its shadow over Muleshoe.

She had seen the lines deepen in Uncle Benton's face and noticed the worry sharpen in her father's eyes.

They had called the Baron a crackpot when the first posters had appeared. But then the raids had begun, the name was no longer taken lightly and people ceased laughing. The terror was not confined to Muleshoe. It had spread all along the borders of this wild stretch of country, called the Escalante because it sloped upward into the dry plateaus of Mexico.

She had the sticky feeling that Tom Benton was out in that wild country, hurt and lost and looking for something he wouldn't find. The thought brought on a helpless feeling she couldn't shake off.

Ruth had always admired and loved her Uncle Tom. He was a big man, strong and sure of himself, and he had laughed often. She had known him like this as a child, for Tom Benton had never married; he had lived with the Dillmans from the day they had come to Muleshoe. Ruth had come to look upon him as a second father—and sometimes with even more affection than she gave her own father, for Sam was often preoccupied and harassed and had little time for her.

It was Tom Benton who taught her to ride, opened up the beauties of the desert hills, told her stories of this country, of old trails and older days when Texas had been a Spanish province. . . .

"I'll trade you pennies for your thoughts," a man's voice interrupted. There was a trace of dry humor in the voice.

She started and looked up into Solitary Jackson's unsmiling eyes.

The Ranger was a big man, she noticed, as big as her uncle. He loomed over her, a solid figure in the early morning. Yet there was a remoteness in this man that was like a shell built layer upon layer over some inner and totally different facet of personality.

She put her troubled glance on him. "I'm afraid they're not worth trading," she said. "I was thinking of Uncle Tom."

He lifted his eyes from her face, as though he,

too, felt impelled to search the far distances of the desert. His face was grave.

"Your uncle's an old hand in this country, Ruth. I think he knows what he's doing."

"But to ride out alone — in that storm. And at night —"

"He wasn't alone," Jackson interrupted. "He had a hardcase named Holt with him."

Her eyes darkened. "Holt?"

He nodded. "A gunman from up San Saba way. Claimed he was a stranger in Muleshoe. Came in on yesterday's stage." He shrugged. "He gave me trouble and I locked him in your uncle's cell. Last night Tom Benton broke into the office. Holt was gone when I looked in. I reckon your uncle took him with him."

Ruth was confused. "Why? What reason would Uncle Tom have for taking this gunman with him?"

Jackson looked past her, into the desert hills. "I don't know. I can only guess, Ruth. I think this San Saba gunslinger was Bob Crane's brother. I think Tom Benton found out."

"It doesn't make sense to me," she said. "Even if this man was Bob's brother, what could he have known of what's out in the desert?"

"Maybe nothing," he said shortly. He didn't want to hurt her. But Tom Benton was not rational, and so it was impossible to understand his motives.

She turned and looked at the desert. There was a clearness to the morning that made the distant mountains stand out like gray-blue etchings.

"Beautiful, isn't it? Hard to believe that anything so beautiful can be so cruel . . ."

"I've found they sometimes go together," Jackson murmured. "The beautiful and the cruel."

Ruth Dillman reacted to this with a woman's instinct. She turned and searched his face, looking for a clue to the bleak cynicism in this big man.

"You're not a happy man, Mr. Jackson?"

"Jim," he said. "Though it's been twenty years since I heard a woman call me that —" His eyes had a dark hurt in them, a brief and involuntary chink in his reserve.

"I was nine years old," he said. His voice was flat. "My mother, my father, and my two older sisters were killed by Comanches. The last thing my mother said was 'Run, Jim — run!' " He was silent a moment, caught in the buried tragedy of the past. "They caught me, anyway, down by the river. I don't know why they didn't kill me. A month later an Apache war party ran into us, killed the Comanches and took me with them. I lived with them for five years. . . ."

Ruth put a hand on his arm. Her fingers were warm and, looking down, he saw a tenderness in her eyes, a physical awareness of him.

"You haven't answered me, Jim. Are you a happy man?"

He considered this. No woman had shown this

much concern for him, or come so close to penetrating the shell he had built up. He tried to see this with perspective. . . .

She was a woman grown, and possibly tired of this desert town. He represented a change. But she didn't know what it would mean, and he was reluctant to change his own life. He viewed this coldly. He had never been an impulsive man. And he saw that it wouldn't work, nor would it be fair to this girl to let her think otherwise.

"No," he admitted. "Not always. But life isn't a matter of personal happiness, Ruth. Maybe I've knocked around too much. One of the penalties of growing old, I reckon, is that the shine rubs off of things." He grinned at her, his eyes taking her lightly, and she saw this and it hurt.

"Of course," she said quickly, withdrawing within her own shell. "I guess I'm just moody this morning, Jim. I've had a bad night, worrying about Uncle Tom."

"A good breakfast might help," Jackson suggested. "Funny how a full stomach sometimes changes a man's perspective."

"I've had my breakfast," she replied. "But I'm sure you must be hungry. I'll have bacon and eggs for you before you finish your first cup of coffee."

She turned quickly, not wanting him to see her face.

Red Davis was sober. And when he was sober he was a poor hand at the type cases. His hands trembled violently as he worked and his Adam's apple kept bobbing in his scrawny throat as though he was having a hard time swallowing. He looked like a fish out of water.

Phil Petersen came out of his office with copy in his hand. "We'll set this under a forty-eight-point banner head, Red —"

Davis started. He bumped his elbow against the bench and dropped the stick he held in his left hand. Type scattered over the floor.

Petersen whirled on him, temper flaring across his thin face. "What in the devil's the matter with you? You've been jumpy all morning!"

"I need a drink," Davis whined. "I'm no good without a drink."

"You're not much good drunk, either!" Petersen snapped. "I don't know why I keep you here."

"I — I need a drink," Davis repeated sullenly. He didn't look at Petersen, but his mutter reached the publisher. "And you need me, all right —"

They both turned as the front doorbell jangled.

Petersen stepped away from the type cases. "Good morning, Jackson," he greeted coldly. "What can I do for our new town marshal?"

"I want to talk with your man Davis," the Ranger said curtly. "I've got something he lost."

Petersen frowned. He called Davis over. "Ranger looking for you, Red."

Davis shuffled over, reluctantly, like a cur

approaching another dog's bone.

Solitary Jackson held out the notebook Judd had dropped. "This yours?"

Davis started to put his hand out for it, then drew it back quickly. "No," he muttered. "Never owned a notebook."

Jackson said quietly, "Look it over, Red. You might remember having lost it."

Davis kept his hand behind his back. He shook his head. "Never owned a notebook! Never lost one!" His voice was dogged. He glanced at Petersen in silent appeal.

Petersen stepped forward. "Where'd you get this, Ranger? What's in it that's important?"

"An old newspaper clipping," Solitary answered. "I thought Davis might be able to explain it."

Petersen held out his hand. "Mind if I have a look at it?"

"Not at all." Jackson watched Petersen read the news item, studying the man's thin, arrogant face.

"Where's the rest of the clipping?"

"That's all that was in the notebook," Jackson replied evenly. "Judd gave it to me last night — just before he was killed. He said your man here, Davis, lost it when he slept off a drunk in the barn the other night."

"Judd's a liar!" Davis shouted. "It ain't my notebook."

"Judd's dead," Jackson reminded him coldly.

Petersen handed the notebook back. "What

does it mean?" His voice held a small curiosity. "What's all the fuss about? Far as I can make out it's an old news story concerning Governor Coke and a man named Duncan Stafford."

"I was hoping Davis could tell me more about it."

"I don't know anything about that notebook or the clipping," Davis snarled. He backed away from them, his face twitching. "Sure I slept in Selwick's barn the other night. But I didn't lose that book!"

Jackson shrugged. "It doesn't take much courage to call a dead man a liar," he pointed out. He turned to leave.

"Just a minute, Jackson!" Petersen's voice held a flat anger. "Amos Selwick told me this morning about Judd being killed. I heard other stories, too. I learned that Tom Benton's left town. That he broke into the law office, busted into that back-room cell and took that red-headed gunslinger with him."

Jackson's smile was wintry. "You've been getting around, I see."

"It's my job," Petersen snapped. "The *Chronicle* comes out in two days." He shook his finger at Jackson, like an irate teacher scolding a pupil. "You want to know what's in this week's editorial, Jackson?"

The Ranger shrugged. "I'll read it later," he said bleakly and started for the door.

"I'll tell you anyway!" Petersen snarled. "It's about you, Jackson! All about you! How you lived with the Apaches for five years. How you turned on Lame Coyote when he took to the warpath some years ago. Led an Army cavalry company against him. Killed a riverboat gambler in New Orleans. Hunted down Ben Ambers for the five-thousand-dollar reward on his head. Brought him back dead, didn't you, Jim?"

Jackson turned. His eyes were a curious smoky gray. "Jim? Not many men know me by my first name, Petersen."

Petersen's lips twitched. "I told you I know a lot about you. It's my job to know."

"This is a hard country," Jackson said slowly. His jaw was rigid, iron-cast. "But there's nothing I've done I'm ashamed of. I don't have to apologize to you for anything."

"Not to me perhaps," Petersen sneered. "But that Dillman girl won't like what she'll read. And maybe some of the fools who've listened to Tom Benton spout about you might change their minds when they read the *Chronicle*."

Jackson searched the newspaperman's arrogant face. "I thought it was the Baron who was giving this town trouble," he said obliquely.

"I'm not afraid of the Baron," Petersen said. "I'm not afraid of you, either, Ranger. I just don't like you, or any of Captain MacDonald's boys. The Frontier Battalion! Hah!" He almost spat out his distaste. "A bunch of killers riding in the name of Texas law and order! A man brings his own gun and his own horse and rides for Texas on forty a month. Don't make me laugh,

Jackson. He rides for what's in it for him — the way you do. Ben Ambers meant five thousand dollars to you, didn't he? That's what you pin that badge on for, isn't it?"

Jackson shook his head. "Someone must have treated you pretty badly," he muttered.

"Not as badly as I'm going to treat you!" Petersen shouted. "You're going to be glad to leave town once I get through with you. I'm going to show the folks in Muleshoe just what kind of a man you really are. You came to town and made a great show of taking over. But Judd Viers was killed right under your nose by some killer with a bow —"

"A crossbow, Petersen. A madman using a weapon he must have picked up in some museum —"

It stopped the tall, gaunt man for a moment. His face went stiff and his eyes searched the Ranger's face. "A crossbow?"

Jackson nodded. "No Indian ever built an arrow like the one you showed me, or that which killed Judd. It came from a crossbow. You ought to have known, Petersen. There's a madman in town, not out in the desert. And when I find that bow I'll have the man behind all this trouble —"

"We know who's behind the trouble." Petersen's voice was stiff. "The problem appears to be what you're doing about it."

"All I can," Jackson snapped. He put his gaze squarely on Petersen. "I might be able to do more, with your help. But you seem convinced

I'm only in the way here. You seem to blame me for Judd's death, for Tom Benton's leaving town. But I haven't seen you or any of Muleshoe's frightened citizens do anything about Judd or Tom Benton or Bob Crane. Benton was the only man to write for help from the Rangers —"

"He didn't care much for that help, judging from the way he acted when you showed up," Petersen sneered. "I'd say he had reason."

"Perhaps," Jackson answered coldly. "Some day I'll find out why Tom Benton tried to kill me."

"I told you yesterday what I am going to do," Petersen added harshly. "This is a matter for the governor himself. I plan to hold an open meeting the day he arrives. This is his problem. I'm going to ask for the state militia, not the Rangers."

Jackson sighed wearily and turned away. Petersen waved the copy he held in his hand.

"Just a minute, Ranger. I always give equal space to anyone I oppose in my paper. Have you any statement to make for the next edition of the *Chronicle*?"

Jackson looked back. A bleak humor lightened his eyes.

"Why sure," he said softly. "I've got a statement for you, Petersen. Put it in a box on the front page. Say that Ranger Solitary Jackson promises to smash the Escalante bunch within the week. Write that he will have the Baron in jail by the time Governor Coke shows up in Muleshoe. Print that, Petersen!"

Petersen laughed harshly. He watched the big lawman step out and close the door behind him. Then he turned to face Davis.

The printer was edging toward the back door. His lined, dirty face held beads of sweat. Petersen took a step after him and the man cringed and lifted a hand as if to ward off a blow. Then he whirled and darted out the door. . . .

XII

Amos Selwick, looking slovenly and ill at ease in bib overalls, was sweeping out the stable when Jackson walked in.

Selwick had come to work early, after a sleepless night and an uneasy breakfast. The picture of Judd's body haunted him. Even after Zoe Walker, the undertaker, had taken Judd away the fear had stayed with him. He had left the stables immediately, locked himself in his quarters and pulled down all the shades. He had sweated through the close heat of the night, and morning had found him convinced he was through with Muleshoe.

Yet he resented his decision. He had made a comfortable living here. Amos was a man who demanded little of life. A few good friends, a place to sleep, good food. And Muleshoe had offered him that. Women had never troubled him. Amos had early decided that they gave more trouble than pleasure.

But he was frightened now, and his fear sought outlet in a sullen resentment that found a ready focus in this big Ranger. Tom Benton had led most of the citizens in Muleshoe to expect wonders from this man, and to his way of thinking

Solitary Jackson had not measured up to expectations at all.

Now he laid his broom aside and wiped his forehead with a blue handkerchief he pulled out of his hip pocket. He kept his gaze averted as Jackson walked to the stall where his roan was tethered. Then his voice lifted with querulous insinuation.

"You pay Judd last night?"

Jackson turned and put a long hard glance on the fat man. He caught the hostility in Amos and it rankled. He realized he had started off on the wrong foot here when he had been forced to defend himself against Tom Benton. He had antagonized Phil Petersen, who seemed to be a power in Muleshoe. And he had been powerless to prevent Judd's death.

These were the things Muleshoe's citizens would remember. Phil Petersen would never let them forget. A bitter seam opened up in Jackson's face as he recalled the publisher's threats. There was nothing in his past Jackson was ashamed of. But Petersen could twist the facts, shift the emphasis, so that the majority of his readers would get a distorted picture.

He saw Selwick lick his lips, gathering courage to repeat his question, and he forestalled the man.

"I usually pay my bill when I leave," he said coldly. "And I expect to be in town for some time, Amos."

Selwick leaned on his broom, his mouth sullen. "You'll have to find another place for your horse, Ranger. I'm closing up." He gestured to a cardboard sign he had propped against the wall: *For Sale, Cheap.*

"I'm quitting Muleshoe," he added.

Jackson studied this soft man. He was the type, he thought, the kind that started running at the first real trouble.

"Any other livery in town?"

"Nope."

Jackson frowned. "This sort of puts me in a spot, Amos. I don't fancy leaving my cayuse out nights."

"Not my problem," Amos muttered. "I'm selling the business. Soon as I find some fool with money —"

"Reckon he'll need more than money, won't he?" Jackson's voice held a bright anger. "He'll need a little guts, too."

Amos flushed. "All he'll need is money," he muttered. "And not too much of it, either. But he'd be a blamed fool to stay in Muleshoe after the trouble we've been having."

Jackson held back his contempt. There was no arguing with this man. He was ready to run, and he wouldn't be the last.

"I'll pay you a week in advance. Until you find a buyer."

Amos shook his head. "I don't want the bother, Ranger. Judd did all the work here."

"I'll take care of my cayuse myself."

Amos stroked his chin, his eyes reluctant. "All right," he assented. "Suit yourself. But I won't be held responsible for anything that might happen."

"Don't expect you to." Jackson started to leave, then remembered why he had come here. He held out the notebook Judd had dropped.

"I saw Davis at the *Chronicle*," he explained shortly. "Davis said he didn't lose it. Claims he never owned a notebook. Might as well put it away with the rest of Judd's belongings."

Selwick closed his fingers over the book. He watched Jackson leave, then he slipped the book into his pocket without glancing through it. He picked up the cardboard sign, found a hammer and half a dozen rusting tacks, and started to nail the sign to the door.

In the morning light Jackson examined the bullet-torn lock on the law office door. The door was partially open, seeming to mock him. If anyone else had been curious enough to come up here and look around, Jackson saw no signs.

He turned and looked back along the hot, sandy street to the town. It had no discernible pattern. Half a dozen alleys wandered off from the main street and behind the warped board fronts sprawled sheds, fenced lots, and a haphazard collection of private dwellings.

Looming up behind Muleshoe was the gray-brown bulk called Hopeful Ridge, pockmarked with mining shafts. Several of the mines were still in operation, and it was this factor which had brought Muleshoe into existence and kept it alive. This, and the plain fact that between this town and Concho, almost seventy miles away, there was nothing save an occasional squatter's shack housing some hardy soul with a love of solitude and a hatred of people.

It was late morning and the blazing sun forced its lethargy over Muleshoe. Jackson had a moment's wonder at what Ruth Dillman saw in it. There seemed to be nothing here for a woman except the dismal prospect of a shabby life. Yet Ruth saw more; perhaps she saw it with the freshness of hope.

The desert was a cruel, desolate wasteland to most. Yet to some it held beauty, and to others it was a haven.

The Baron and his men found the Escalante friendly. Somewhere in that barren, burning stretch of sand and twisted rock they had found a refuge from which they mocked the authority of Texas, terrorized settlers along the desert's perimeter, and vanished without a trace.

One aspect of this puzzled Jackson. For all the bizarre nature of the Baron's demands, there seemed little hope of any economic gain. And Jackson had learned that few men did anything without some end in mind. For most it was money. And yet . . .

Even supposing that the Baron would be allowed to keep this stretch of wasteland, what would it gain him? Perhaps, to a madman, it would be enough. A warped ego might be content to occupy and rule a desert empire that had no value.

But somehow Jackson had the feeling there was more to it than this. He had the hunch that the whole mad scheme had been planned to a more narrow, personal end. He had this hunch, and it nagged at him.

Perhaps the key to it all lay out there in the desert. Tom Benton had known something, before the bullet had addled his memory. Bob Crane, obviously, had known. And Tom Benton had come to his office last night to recover something he had left there. Taking Holt with him might have been nothing more than an afterthought.

But what could Tom Benton have been after?

Jackson walked inside. Last night's storm had left a thin layer of sand across the floor. His boots crunched on it. He walked to the cell door and looked inside, then turning, he was held by the tobacco scattered beyond the door.

He could find no reason for this, unless Tom Benton had come back for his tobacco — or something he had hidden inside the tobacco tin.

Jackson shrugged. He could get this far with his assumptions, but they brought him no nearer to what he wanted to know.

He stepped out, closing the door behind him. He gazed at the low hills fading into the desert heat haze. Benton was out there with Marvey Holt. Early this morning he had half-expected to see Benton and Holt come trailing back to town.

He had told Ruth Dillman this, while having breakfast, now his reassurances had a hollow echo.

For what it would be worth, he decided, he'd take a ride out there and have his look around. . . .

He was in the Oro Grande Saloon, asking guarded questions, when George Vollmer looked in and saw him at the bar. It was eleven o'clock, and the heat was beginning to dissipate the lingering coolness inside the saloon. The stage line manager elbowed up beside the Ranger and asked what Jackson was drinking. He ordered the same, drank his first shot fast, and ordered refills.

"I've got your driver," he said. "We can start any time after noon today."

"We?" Jackson's tone was curious.

George flushed. "I've got to get that bullion shipment to Harrisburg," he reminded, "or I might lose my job. If you're willing to ride shotgun then I'm willing to drive!"

Jackson smiled. "I see your point." He held up his glass. "Let's drink to it."

Vollmer drained his glass. "Just for the record, Ranger," he muttered. "Why are you risking your neck on this trip?"

Jackson considered this. "A man can hunt a big cat for days and never find where he holes up. Stake some bait out though, and the chances are two to one he'll have the big cat under his sights by nightfall."

"I see what you mean." Vollmer nodded. He poured one more round.

"Let's hope we see the big cat first, eh?"

XIII

Ruth Dillman hung her apron on a hook in the kitchen and stepped out the side door. The heat of the day flushed her face. She felt hot and disturbed. She knew her father was worried, too.

Tom Benton had often ridden out into the desert. He was an oldtimer here, and he was familiar with the country. He could have headed for a half-dozen places he knew about in the Escalante.

But Tom Benton was not now the same man who had told her of the old, abandoned mining towns and prospector's shacks out in the desert.

She stared into the heat haze at the end of the street, wanting to believe Jackson. But inside her the knot of fear grew.

Her father had tried to get up a search party, but no one had listened to him.

"Tom'll be back, Sam," they told him. "Heck, Tom ain't no fool . . . even if . . ." They had flushed, most of them, and refrained from saying what they knew.

Ruth shaded her aching eyes against the glare from the hot hills. She turned her face away and, doing this, knew she had to look for Uncle Tom. All her life she had looked up to him. He was the other side of Sam — the side her father could not be — the glamorous side. Tom Benton had time for her when Sam did not; she had gone to him with her childhood troubles and he had understood.

She thought of Jim Jackson. He was like Tom Benton, younger, more grave than her uncle, though — and somehow harder. A man driven. There was something about Jackson that held people at a distance, an aloofness about him that discouraged intimacy.

Solitary Jackson. The nickname fitted him. And then she remembered that he had lived as an Apache during his formative years. A boy, still shocked by the massacre of his parents and sisters, raised in an Apache camp.

Some understanding of the man came to her then. And some of the bitterness that had crept into his voice, as he ate breakfast, could be forgiven.

"I've got a job to do, Ruth," he had told her. "I'm no superman. I was ordered here to look into things, find out how much truth there was to this Baron story. I was told to contact Muleshoe's marshal, your uncle . . ." His eyes had a remote hardness. "I found what I came after. I could leave now, make my report back at Company Headquarters. But I'm stubborn. I want to find out why your uncle tried to kill me when I told him who I was. And I want to find the man who killed Judd."

She knew Jackson would ride into the desert, if

she asked him again. But he didn't know the country; he would have little idea of where to start looking for Tom Benton.

There was one place Uncle Tom had often talked of. The old mining town of Dawson's Gulch. She had been there with him several times — she knew the way.

She made up her mind then, knowing she would find little rest until she tried. She wouldn't tell Sam. Her father would never let her go. If she hurried she could be back before the supper-hour rush.

She went back inside. Sam was cleaning the range. She said, "I'm going to visit with Mabel Whiting, Dad. Think you can spare me this afternoon?"

Sam put a quick, searching glance on her. He nodded. "Have a good time, Ruth. I'll get young Timmy to help me out with the noon rush."

She took the path through the back lot, crossed the gully behind, and came out on the side road leading to the Whiting house. Mabel was married to Mark Whiting, who worked in the general store. She was a few years older than Ruth, and at the moment was pregnant again, her third child in four years.

Ruth stayed long enough to have coffee and appease her conscience. Then she left and headed for Selwick's stables. She came by the back way and missed Jackson by a scant two minutes. She found Amos about to close up.

She read the For Sale sign on the door and

curiosity prompted her. "You planning to leave Muleshoe, Sam?"

"As soon as I can," he muttered defiantly. "Town ain't a fit place for decent folks any more."

She caught his meaning. "But you can't run," she protested. "We can't all run just because a madman is loose —"

"I'm not running," Amos said. But he said it shamefacedly. "I just don't feel there's anything in Muleshoe to keep me. Look what happened to your uncle Tom. To Judd. And what does anyone do about it? Tom Benton wrote to Austin for help, didn't he? And they send one man —"

"Mr. Jackson's doing all he can," she said. "If more people would help him instead of looking at him as though *he* was the enemy, there might be no need to run."

"Help him?" Amos looked indignant. "What has he done since he got here? Shot your uncle, put a stranger in jail and crippled Nick Cates. I never liked Nick Cates, Ruth. But he ain't one of the Baron's men. And last night he gets Judd killed —" Amos shook his head. "If that's the kind of protection we've got, I'm glad to be leaving."

Ruth made a helpless gesture. "I'm sorry you feel that way, Amos." She turned to the stalls. "I came to hire a horse. I want to ride today. First nice day we've had in a week."

Amos looked troubled. "I'm closing up, Ruth. Besides, your uncle took Nig and the bay mare."

A whining note crept into his voice. "Don't expect I'll ever get repaid —"

"If Uncle Tom doesn't bring them back, Dad'll see you get paid for them!" Ruth said. She had lost patience with the soft, complaining man. "And if you want to get paid now —"

"Aw, forget it, Ruth. Take the roan — No, not that big fellow. Belongs to that Ranger. The one over by the window. Here, I'll saddle her for you. . . ."

Five minutes later Ruth Dillman rode out of Muleshoe. She left by the side road and few people saw her. The sun was a blazing ball of fire overhead.

Out of town she turned the mare to the north, toward the lost mining town of Dawson's Gulch.

The sun beat down over the Dawson's Gulch road, pouring heat into the long-deserted canyon gold camp. On each side of the narrow ribbon of road the scarred slopes lifted, raw and ugly and speckled with ore dumps.

Twenty years ago a thousand men had worked these diggings and the town of Dawson's Gulch had flourished. Now little was left of the hopes and dreams of those thousand men except a few sagging shacks and abandoned holes.

In the concealing shadows of the live oak clump at the bend of the road, where it dipped down to the mining camp, four men waited with stolid patience.

One of them was "Two-Bit" Jones, the breed

who had signaled from the shoulder of Iron Butte. Jones worked as a swamper and handyman for the Oro Grande; he was an inconspicuous man whose comings and goings in Muleshoe generally went unnoticed.

The other three were from the desert hideout of the Escalante raiders.

Jode Slade pinched the butt of his cigarette between powerful fingers and let it fall. He was a big-shouldered man with a dark cruel face — a man wanted for murder in Dodge City and Abilene and other trail towns. Most of the county sheriffs in Texas had dodgers on Slade in their wanted files.

He was lounging in saddle of a big black stallion with a blaze face, and a star was pinned boldly to his black cotton shirt. He had taken it from the body of a Ranger he had killed. He did not often wear it, but this was a special occasion. He fingered it with cruel anticipation.

Two-Bit glanced at the high-riding sun. "They come pretty quick, I think." He looked at Jode. "Boss say no kill Jackson. Take him to hideout."

Jode didn't listen. He was thinking that he was getting tired of taking the Baron's orders, getting fed up with the man's grandiose schemes. He had a pretty good idea why the Baron wanted Jackson taken prisoner. The Baron was thinking of Little Bear; the flat-nosed Apache leader was getting restless.

As far as Jode was concerned Little Bear and

his warriors could clear out any time. But he knew how the Baron felt.

He waited, hunched in saddle, taking the heat with the patience of a desert hawk. Two or three more good hauls like the Daylight Special holdup and the Baron could go hang.

The tough blond rider on his right suddenly straightened. "Someone's coming," he murmured, and reached for the rifle under his left leg.

Jode's voice held a lazy warning: "I'll handle him, Potter. I've been waiting a long time to brace this Ranger. . . ."

Ruth Dillman searched the scarred slopes. The heat was caught in the steep-walled canyon and she felt the beat of the sun on her head and it made her slightly dizzy.

She knew better than to come riding without a hat. But she had not taken time to change; Mother would have wanted to know where she was riding, and this venture would have been immediately discouraged.

She let the roan mare take her pace toward the cluster of shacks at the head of the canyon. At any moment she expected someone to step out into the blazing street. But nothing moved along the sand-covered walks, and the glassless windows were like unseeing eyes in the face of this dead town.

Disappointment made her want to cry. If Tom Benton was here he'd have seen her by this time.

He would have come out —

She saw the rider move out of the oak clump, and a cry of relief came to her lips — and died there. The big man on the black horse was not Tom Benton. He was not anyone she had ever seen before.

She felt fear chill her; she had a sudden impulse to swing the tired mare around and make a run for it.

Jode Slade pulled up in front of her, and now she saw the star of Texas on his black shirt and the desert dust clinging to his wide shoulders. He ran his eyes over her, like probing fingers, bold and searching.

"Looking for someone, gal?"

He was wearing a badge, but he was no lawman. She was sure of it without knowing why. Something about the way he looked at her, at the way he waited, something cold and cruel in the patient question.

She shook her head. Her gaze lifted to the two other riders who came straggling down from the oaks. She knew now they had been waiting there.

For her? They could not have known she was coming.

"No." She tried to keep a rising panic out of her voice. "I — I just came out for the ride."

"In the midday heat? Dressed like that?" Jode was grinning at her.

She didn't see Two-Bit until he rode up behind her. He edged up beside Jode and put his stolid gaze on Ruth.

"She's Tom Benton's niece, Jode."

Ruth stared at him. The other two had come up by this time; they flanked her, silent and menacing.

She had seen Jones in town, but had paid little attention to him. She realized now that evasion would get her nowhere.

"I'm looking for my uncle," she admitted. "He isn't well. He left town last night, during the height of the storm."

"You thought he came here?" Anticipation glinted briefly in Jode Slade's eyes.

"I hoped so," she replied. "He sometimes came here with me. I thought, with the way things were last night, he wouldn't try to ride far. He would need some place where he could take shelter —"

Jode turned to the two men flanking her. "Potter — you an' Lefty take a look. Search every one of the shacks. Make damn sure Tom Benton isn't in one of them!"

Something in his tone piled up alarm in Ruth. She started to edge her mare away.

"I'll help look," she said. "He might not act friendly if he sees strangers."

Jode grinned. He edged his black in close and reached for the mare's bridle. "Take it easy," he advised. "Potter an' Lefty will take good care of your uncle — if they run across him."

She didn't protest. She felt the fear grow in her, numbing her thoughts. Her eyes moved past Jode to the two men who had dismounted up the street in Dawson's Gulch and were searching each sagging shack, gun in hand. She felt trapped and her fear beat inside her, like a bird in a cage.

Two-Bit backed his cayuse away from them. His impassive face was shadowed by the brim of his huge hat.

"I go look from hill," he told Jode. His voice was as colorless as his face was bland. "Stage should come soon."

Jode nodded. He ran his eyes over Ruth again, and her face flamed. She jerked on her reins.

"It's hot in the sun. I should have taken a hat along —"

"It's cooler in the shade," he admitted. Without releasing his hold on her bridle, he turned his back. The roan mare followed willingly as he led the way to the oak clump.

The coolness was immediate as they entered the dappled shade. A faint breeze fanned her flushed face. She felt the brief pull of hope as Jode dropped his hand from her bridle and swiveled in his saddle. He watched Two-Bit climb the opposite slope, dismount, disappear between two huge, rust-colored rock outcroppings and appear on the other side.

He waved his hat at Jode almost immediately and ducked back behind the rocks.

Jode's big hand went down to his right Colt, lifted it. His voice held a harsh warning.

"We're gonna have company, gal. When I tell you, you'll ride down to the road. Don't do anything or say anything. Just ride down to that road an' wait. . . ."

She looked at his face, at the gun in his hand. The click of the hammer under his thumb sent a shudder through her. She nodded dumbly.

XIV

Solitary Jackson watched the road unwind ahead of the stage. The sun glared on the white alkali bottoms and the heat waves shimmered over the twin ruts. Ahead of them a jack rabbit broke from the shade of a mesquite bush and went loping toward the sand hills.

The Ranger sat loose on the jolting seat, a hard, grim man with a rifle held easily across his knees.

The stage carried no passengers. None had been willing to book passage when it was known they would be hauling bullion. For the past six months few shipments of value had been safe from the Escalante raiders.

Jackson watched the road through slitted eyes, a big man seemingly unconcerned with anything that might happen. But a small, nagging voice was beginning to bother him.

He had let the town's apparent hostility goad him into a move that held little promise. More and more he was sure that the answer to what he was after was in Muleshoe — that the big game he hunted was not interested in the bullion.

But he had to go through with it now. He had put himself up as bait for the Escalante raiders, gambling that it would bring the self-proclaimed ruler of Deserta out into the open.

Up ahead the road forked. The trail swinging south went through low rocky hills and seemed little used.

George Vollmer swung the stage onto this road.

Jackson turned his attention to the stocky man on the seat. "This the regular road to Harrisburg?"

Vollmer shook his head. He seemed tense, nervous. He had talked little since leaving Muleshoe. Still, under the circumstances, it seemed natural.

"Rough road, but shorter this way," he explained. "Goes through the old gold camp of Dawson's Gulch. There's water there we can use — won't be another stopover until we hit Badwater Station." He grinned nervously. "If they got wind of this shipment, they'll be looking for us on the main road, Jackson. This ought to throw them off."

Jackson settled back. The explanation was glib, but he remained alert, suspicion narrowing his gaze. He kept his eyes on the slopes. . . .

An hour later they drove through the narrow canyon walls into Dawson's Gulch. Jackson's gaze caught the meaning of the sagging shacks up ahead . . . the deserted street . . . the higher walls hemming this small lost town.

Dead end!

Then he saw the rider come down the slope to

the road, and he slammed his foot on the brake and swung his rifle up. The stage wheels locked and the coach slewed sideways in the sandy ruts. George Vollmer cursed.

But Jackson sat stiffly, his face bleak in the reflected glare of the sun.

The rider pulling to a stop on the road was Ruth Dillman!

He lifted his foot from the brake and his voice held a harsh wonder: "Drive easy, George. Something's wrong."

Ruth rode down to the road. She didn't look at the stage, at Jackson. She pulled up between the drifted-over ruts and slumped over her saddle horn. She seemed hurt, or sick.

Alarm whipped caution from Jackson. He called "Ruth!" and laid his rifle on the seat between him and George. He got up and started to turn — The hard muzzle that pressed against his ribs was definite in its deadly warning.

"Sit down, Jackson!" Vollmer's voice was nervously harsh.

Jackson hesitated a bare moment. He had been expecting an ambush. But he had made one bad mistake. He had not figured George Vollmer in this at all.

He sat down slowly and Ruth raised her head. Her eyes seemed to look through him. There was a numb helplessness in the droop of her shoulders. And Jackson saw the reason for this now as Jode Slade broke out of the screening oaks and rode down to meet the stage. Two other riders came into sight from between the empty buildings at the far end of the street and started riding toward him.

Jackson had one brief impulse to make a break. George must have sensed it. The muzzle jerked back from Jackson's ribs and his voice rasped thinly: "Stand up, Ranger! Clasp your hands over your hat!"

Jackson looked at the pearl-handled pistol in the town man's hand. It was of smaller caliber than the Colts in his holsters, but none the less deadly at this close range.

He stood up and locked his fingers over his head.

The two men riding along Dawson's Gulch's empty street and the big man on the white-faced black stud arrived at the stage at the same time. Lefty and Potter had drawn rifles; they waited now, flanking the girl, grinning expectantly.

There was a small slide of pebbles on the other side of the stage. Two-Bit Jones rode down from the opposite slope and pulled up beside Vollmer. He hung back a little from the main group, his black button eyes as inscrutable as glass.

Jode Slade rested his hands on his pommel and ran his gaze over Jackson. The star on his shirt caught the sun and sent out sharp spears of light as he moved.

"So this is the hombre who gunned Nick Cates? Fastest gun in the Frontier Battalion?" He spit into the sand in front of him. "Heard a lot about you, Solitary. Figured you a plumb cagey jasper. Until I see you let a tinhorn like George stick a gun in your ribs!"

Jackson was eyeing the star on the outlaw's shirt. It was the mate to the one he was wearing, and some of the things which had puzzled him began to fall into an understandable pattern.

Jode caught his glance and grinned. "Handy piece of silver," he said, fingering the badge. "Fooled Tom Benton with it. Made him think I was you, Jackson. Even after I shot him he still thought I was you."

He laughed harshly, enjoying his joke. But he enjoyed it alone.

Ruth Dillman looked at him, a growing horror darkening her eyes. Her mare moved restlessly, wanting to get away from the blazing sun, wanting to get back to the shade up the slope.

"You the Baron?" Jackson's voice held a thin puzzlement.

"Naw! I ain't that crazy!" Jode shifted in saddle. "But don't fool yourself, Jackson. No one gives Jode Slade orders. Me and the Baron —"

George Vollmer cut in with sharp impatience. "Quit the gabbing, Jode. The Baron wants Jackson out of the way. Said something about keeping him alive until after the governor's visit. He wants to come out and see the fun —"

Slade's eyes narrowed dangerously. "You giving orders now, George?"

Vollmer caught himself. A flicker of fear appeared in his gaze. "I'm only repeating what I was told," he said. "Take him and let me go."

Jode's eyes lidded. The dark skin pulled tight across his cheekbones. He began to chuckle good-naturedly. "Why sure, George. No need to hold you up. You must be in a hurry." He motioned with his Colt to Jackson.

"George is anxious to get back to the Baron, Ranger. So step down here — *an' step down careful!*"

Solitary put a foot over the side, found the iron footrest, and came down. Slade kneed his black up close.

"Unbuckle your gunbelts an' let them fall free!"

Jackson reached for his buckle. He saw Slade start to lean over him, caught the beginning of Ruth's scream. He tried to duck back, and his hands made an instinctive grab for his guns.

Jode's palmed Colt slammed down across his head.

Jackson's legs buckled. His right hand came up in reflex motion; he was falling as he fired a shot into the ground under the big black's fore-feet.

Slade cursed as the animal jumped, nearly unseating him. He pulled the stallion's head down in a savage burst of strength that brought blood frothing to the horse's mouth. His Colt swung around to the Ranger. But Jackson lay face down on the road, unmoving. His hat had rolled free and a stray breeze ruffled his dark hair.

Ruth sawed at her reins and tried to break free. Lefty caught the mare's bridle, and Slade's rage-thickened voice snarled: "Shoot her if she tries that again!"

Lefty reached out and backhanded Ruth across the mouth. Her eyes flashed and Lefty slapped her again. She tipped in the saddle, her head rolling; specks of blood showed on her lower lip. She stared at Lefty now through hate-glazed eyes.

George was gripping the reins, holding the frightened team. His face had gone white. He was used to violence, but the viciousness of these men shook him.

He avoided the girl's eyes. He knew what she must be thinking; he had been a respected citizen in Muleshoe, considered by the matrons with daughters as a highly eligible bachelor.

He had liked this girl, but not enough to hold him to Muleshoe. And not enough, now, to risk his neck for her. He didn't know why she was here, but he was thinking of his own skin now. Ruth Dillman would have to take care of herself.

He looked at Slade, his uneasiness showing. "I've done my part," he said. There was little force in his voice. "I'll be driving on now."

Slade put his black across the road in front of the stage. "Going where, George?"

The blood drained from Vollmer's normally ruddy face. He glanced at the others, seeking support and finding none in the hard faces.

"I made a deal with the Baron," he said harshly. "I promised to get Jackson out here for you. In return I was to keep what's in the strongbox —"

"A nice deal," Slade interrupted. "But I didn't make it, George. And besides —" he was grinning as he lifted the muzzle of his Colt — "it's way too much money for you!"

Vollmer saw it coming. He made a lunge for the pistol he had laid on the seat beside him.

Slade's first shot caught him under the left ear. The second went through his neck.

The team lunged forward as George's fingers slackened on the reins. Slade crowded the leaders; he holstered his still-smoking Colt and used both hands to hold the near animal.

"Hold them quiet!" he snarled at Potter and Lefty. "Two-Bit — you keep an eye on the girl!"

Freed of the necessity of holding the team, Jode rode alongside the seat. He reached up and pulled Vollmer's body off and climbed up in George's place. He found the square iron box under the seat. His shoulder muscles bunched under his dusty shirt as he pulled it out, lifted it, set it on the edge of the seat.

"Here. Let go that cayuse an' take this, Lefty. That big dun of yours can carry the weight of this bullion for a couple of miles. Then we'll bury it an' come back for it later."

Lefty rode up close. His dun horse snorted at the weight of the iron box and backed away, shaking his head.

Jode stepped into the saddle of his black and moved alongside the girl. Two-Bit was eyeing the big outlaw from the other side of the stage.

"Me go now?"

Jode shrugged. "Tell the Baron I'll keep Jackson for him. But he better show up soon. I don't know how long I'll be able to hold Little Bear an' his boys in check."

Two-Bit nodded. He edged his cayuse away and kept the stage between him and Slade as he rode away.

Jackson stirred. Slade dismounted and bent over him. He dug his hands into the Ranger's shoulders and pulled him up, then he jammed his Colt against the lawman's sore ribs. Jackson's eyes were still glazed, but he reacted with sudden violence. His right hand came up in a solid smash that rocked the outlaw back on his heels. He stumbled for him, still only partially conscious, a savage instinct for survival pushing him.

Slade drew and nearly fired; he held himself on the thin edge of indecision. Jackson lunged forward. Slade stepped aside and Jackson fell. His hands clawed the hot sand as he started to get up.

Slade booted him in the ribs. "Real tough hombre," he sneered. "I'll give you a chance to get real tough, Jackson. Later. Right now we're traveling!"

Jackson came to his feet. His side ached, and his head was a drum on which a heavy hammer fell at measured intervals.

"Unhitch one of those horses!" Slade ordered. "The bay!"

Jackson swayed on his feet. He could see Ruth slumped over her saddle. Lefty reached out with his free hand to steady the team as Potter worked to unhitch the bay.

"All right, Jackson," Slade taunted. "I heard Apaches can ride anything on four legs. An' you're half 'Pache, ain't you?"

His Colt leveled on the Ranger. "Get up on that bay!"

Jackson looked at him through slitted eyes. His gaze dropped to the guns half buried in the sand between him and the outlaw. The guns he had dropped. He seemed to weigh his decision carefully, weigh it against his own thinning patience. Then he turned and made a motion to the girl.

"Let her go, Slade."

Jode laughed. His muzzle lifted and the shot exploded heavily in the hot silence. The girl jerked.

"Next time I'll put a slug through her head, instead of over it!" Jode snarled. "Get on that cayuse!"

Jackson took a deep breath. He edged the nervous bay close to the stage, climbed painfully up to the seat. The blow on the head had left him with a sick emptiness in his stomach. He set his teeth against the hammering pain and stepped astride the bay, gripping the animal's thick mane.

Slade picked up Jackson's Colts. He thrust one under his belt, tossed the other one up to Potter.

"Turn that stage around," he told Potter. "Head it back for town!"

Potter swung the team about. Slade fired a shot between the legs of the lead animal, and the skittish horse broke into a run. Slade watched the stage take the bend and disappear, then he mounted his black. He kneed the stud alongside Jackson.

"Let's ride, Ranger."

XV

Marvey Holt had given up trying to escape. He lay in the cabin while the day's heat thickened and became a breathless, sapping thing that sucked all moisture from his body. He lay on the bunk and the quiet pressed down on his ears and seemed louder than any noise.

Tom Benton was gone again!

Holt got to his feet and found that the beans and the rest had done wonders for him. He felt stronger, and his step was steady and he was more conscious of the twinge of pain in his side. He walked slowly, still not trusting himself and not wanting to break open the wound again.

He paused in the doorway and looked around. The shack seemed lost under the canyon wall. The two horses dozed in the shade of the ramada. Marvey saw that Tom Benton had gathered some grass somewhere and dropped it in front of the animals, several wisps of it were scattered under them.

The saddles still lay against the cliff wall, but the rifle was gone. Benton was probably crazy some of the time, but he was sane enough to remember this. Holt stepped out into the full beat of the sun and flinched; he found himself suddenly thirsty again.

He turned and walked toward the sound of murmuring water. . . .

Fifty yards past the limestone outcrop was a splotch of green growing close to the canyon wall. Two small trees, wispy in their foliage, cast a thin shade.

Benton was sprawled under one of the trees. Holt studied the long bony frame lying loose in sleep. His hat lay over his eyes, and his breathing was regular. The bandages around his skull were gray as his hair.

Benton was no fool, Holt reflected wryly. This was a better place to catch up on some sleep than inside the stifling cabin. His gaze was drawn to the rifle lying close by Benton's outstretched arm. The man was asleep. And he felt that this time he could move fast enough to outwit the old marshal.

But the morning's conversation with Benton stopped him. Bob Crane had given his life trying to locate the Baron's hideout. He had managed to convey enough information on that slip of paper to give them a good chance of finding it.

Just what Tom Benton intended to do, once they located that desert sanctuary, was not clear. He had that box of dynamite, cached here by the former occupant. But dynamite was a poor weapon against guns. Holt was not familiar with the deadly stuff and he feared it.

He stood a long while in the sun, watching the sleeping marshal. There was respect in his eyes for this leathery, gaunt marshal, more respect than he had given any other man.

He started forward, moving cautiously. His toe brushed a small pebble aside. There was no perceptible movement in Benton to indicate he had heard it. But before his next step was completed Benton's muffled voice asked: "Still figgerin' on makin' a break for it, Holt?"

Holt grinned despite himself. The old marshal was cagey as a desert fox.

"Thought I'd join you, Tom. It was gettin' hotter'n blazes in that shack."

Benton grunted. He pushed his hat off his face and sat up. "Come on — get out of that hot sun, kid. We won't be ridin' for another three, four hours yet."

Holt walked over. He was glad to be in the shade. He guessed that the small rill trickling down from some point in the canyon wall and forming a small pool at its base helped build an illusion of coolness. He lay on his stomach, favoring his side, put his face in the water and drank. The pleasurable coolness reached like a woman's hand down his back; he was reluctant to leave. But he finally sat up and wiped his face with the back of his hand.

"One of the few places in the desert where there's water," Benton said. "Don't ask me how come it's here. There's an old sayin' that water's where you find it in the desert —"

"And the Baron knows where the other spot is," Holt said.

"He knows." Benton's eyes seemed to turn inward. "Probably learned about it from one of those bronco Apaches he's got with him."

Holt frowned. "Who is this Baron, Marshal? What's all the fuss about out here?"

Benton's lips twitched. His eyes grew muddy under his gray bandages. "The Baron? Some crazy fool who got a bunch of killers together and —" He seemed to be trying to focus his thoughts. Some buried fear worked in his face. He kept repeating "Killers," and now his eyes were staring past Holt, looking beyond the canyon walls, to some point in time and space of which he alone knew. . . .

Holt studied the man. There was a pattern to the way Benton seemed to lose touch with reality. Trouble and guns had a way of sending him off.

He said, "Is that why you want the dynamite?"

The blunt question seemed to pull Benton back to the present. He stared at Holt and his eyes were clear.

"Yeah. I got a feelin' it'll come in handy when we find out where they hole up."

Holt made a gesture with his hands. "I don't know anything about that stuff, Tom. It makes me uneasy, just bein' around it. I like something I can hold in my hand, something I know how to handle, like a Colt or that rifle there."

Benton looked at him a long time, his brows furrowed. Then he picked up the rifle and tossed it to Holt. "It's yours."

Holt's fingers curled around the hand-rubbed stock. His eyes met Benton's and he grinned. "Thanks. Makes me feel a lot better."

Benton shrugged. "I swapped talk an' trouble with a heap of gents in my time, kid. You'd make a pretty good lawman some day — if you quit thinkin' about yourself all the time."

Holt's face sobered. The marshal's remark came mighty close to something his brother had once told him. He slid his gaze away from the marshal and gestured vaguely.

"You're all the law I need, Tom. If you say the hombres who killed my brother are out there somewhere, I'm with you."

Benton nodded gravely. "They're out there." He got to his feet. "We'll start riding before sundown. There's a moon tonight, and night is the best time to travel in the desert."

Holt reached for the tobacco sack in his pocket. It was the first time he had felt the urge to smoke since he had come to Muleshoe.

"Maybe we should have let that tough Ranger in with us, Tom. I heard plenty about this hombre Jackson, and he sure lived up to what I heard —"

His hand spilled tobacco and the bag dropped from his fingers. Benton had whirled on him, his hand clawing for his holstered Colt. His eyes were muddy and his face held the stamp of an odd mixture of fear and hate.

"Jackson! Damn you. . . ."

Holt twisted aside just as Benton's gun

cleared. There was a flash and a report and rock powdered on the wall just past Holt's head.

His voice was wild, urgent, as he kept rolling. "Tom! Tom — I'm not Jackson!"

He had the rifle in his hands as he came up in a crouch, but he didn't want to use it. He saw Benton's body stiffen, caught the uncertainty that washed across the old marshal's face.

"It's me, Marvey Holt." There was a cold sweat on Holt's face, and his side pained. "Bob Crane's brother."

Slowly Benton lowered his Colt. He took a step toward Holt. His eyes were slits, peering, as though he was struggling to see through a mist. He scrubbed his face with his left hand. Then he holstered his Colt and turned away. He walked toward the bend in the canyon, to the shack hidden behind it. . . .

Holt lifted a trembling hand to his forehead and brushed cold sweat from it. His legs felt weak again.

He'd have to be mighty careful, he thought. He had to remember that the name of Jackson was taboo.

He settled back on the sparse grass and found his sack of tobacco. And while he built himself another smoke with unsteady hands he speculated on what the big Ranger had done to Tom Benton to produce such a reaction.

They rode at sundown. Thirty minutes later it was night. It came like the closing of some vast silent door, shutting out all daylight. The stars were dimmed by a high-riding cloud haze. And then the moon humped up over the ragged eastern horizon and the world became a ghostly land of humped shadows and pale mysterious reaches.

They rode west, as Bob Crane had written. They rode for three hours. Then Benton pulled up and pointed.

The rock shone in the moonlight, an odd, macabre shape — a skull hanging in the night.

"We'll camp here," Benton decided.

Holt joggled his canteen. It was still full. He had not felt the need of a drink during the ride from Slater's shack. But Skull Rock had no water and he wondered how long they could last with what they had taken along.

He wanted to tell Benton this, but the old marshal seemed lost in his own thoughts, and remembering the incident by the spring Holt was reluctant to question the man.

He dismounted and followed Tom Benton into the thick shadows under the overhanging butte. Benton picketed the black in a coulee shielded by desert shrub, then turned and waited for Holt.

Holt picketed his mare, giving her twenty feet of rope he had found coiled to his saddle. There was scant forage here, but the mare would have to get along with what she could scrounge.

He heard Benton move and watched him. The marshal was climbing the rock, somehow finding footing that brought him up close to the heavy jaw of the strange formation.

From a distance the rock was a skull; up close it was just a mass of sedimentary rock, chiseled by wind and sand.

Holt squatted on his heels and, feeling the burning in his side, decided it would be better to sit. He waited for Benton, but the man was now lost in the deeper shadows.

An uneasy doubt returned to him. Bob Crane might not have meant anything at all with that note he had thrown into the marshal's office. Bob had always liked scribbling verse. Tom Benton might have read into those lines more than Bob intended. They might have to sit here for days, with little water and three cans of beans between them.

He searched the rock's shadows with growing anxiety. Benton was unpredictable. He might just leave him and start walking off into the distance. Holt felt a sudden emptiness in his stomach. He was entirely too dependent on this old marshal.

That wooden box lashed to Benton's saddle made him uneasy, too. There appeared to be enough dynamite in it to blow a town the size of Muleshoe to kingdom come. What possible use could Benton have in mind for that much dynamite?

He heard no warning. But the marshal suddenly appeared, like a shadow out of the darkness. He moved directly to the horses. "Your mare, kid." His voice was a harsh command. "Riders coming."

Holt got up, walked to his horse and clamped a hand over her muzzle. He waited, straining to see in the dark.

It seemed hours before he heard the sound of horses . . . and another hour before shadowy figures rode by. They came within a hundred yards of the rock.

Holt leaned forward, biting back a mutter of surprise.

One of the massed group was a girl. She rode slumped in saddle, and she seemed cold. The other, riding a bay with neither bridle nor saddle, was a big man. A man Holt remembered well. The Ranger who had shot a gun out of his hand, almost broken his jaw, and dumped him into a cell.

There were three other men with them. These he had never seen before. They rode past and faded into the night, and turning, Holt wanted desperately to ask Benton who the girl was.

But the old marshal was staring in the darkness. He was shivering, as though he had the ague. The shine in his eyes made Holt shiver, too, and he choked back his question.

XVI

Jode Slade reached the desert hideout an hour after sunrise. They had ridden all night, stopping only to bury that bullion box they had taken from the stage.

Jode had deliberately taken the long way, riding over malpais and lava beds. No one could have followed him from Dawson's Gulch through the maze of gulleys, barrancas, tortuous paths and pinnacles of fantastic shapes.

The hideout, when they reached it, was one of those geological freaks found in the middle of wasteland. They came to it suddenly, with no warning. The earth seemed to fall away in front of them in steep steps to a cliff-locked valley that held the first patch of green Jackson had seen since Muleshoe. A long adobe building stood naked to the sun, but horses grazed along the small stream shaded by cottonwoods.

Slade pulled up before the forty-foot rock which guarded the trail into the canyon. To his left the canyon rim was strewn with more boulders and narrow fissures splitting toward the valley floor.

Jackson studied the hideout through lidded eyes. As a defensive position, the Ranger calculated, this valley had no value. There was obviously only one way in or out of the canyon: the narrow, switchback trail dropping down in front of them. Two or three men with rifles could bottle the whole crew inside that canyon trap — *if they could find it!*

Jackson glanced at Ruth Dillman. She had ridden without complaint, although the night had chilled enough to penetrate her thin dress. She was sore and tired, but her eyes held little of this as she looked back at him. A faint smile touched her bruised lips.

Jode was searching the overhanging rock; his halloo brought a man into sight on a ledge twenty feet above the trail. A slight figure with a rifle held carelessly across his thighs.

Jode's voice was harsh. "Where in hell were you, Britt?"

Britt shrugged. "Closed my eyes for a second, Jode. Hell, ain't nobody —"

"Some day a slug'll close them permanent!" Jode snarled. "Next time you're caught asleep I'll put one there myself!"

The guard's face grew sullen. He leaned against the rock as Jode and those with him rode on.

The trail down was a dangerous one. The path was so narrow that the horses had to sit on their haunches for most of the way. They came down to the valley floor and rode toward the adobe building, where a group of men straggled toward them.

Jackson lifted his gaze to the canyon rim. The change was fantastic. Down here they seemed to have dropped out of the Llano Escalante. They were in a new world of running water, grass, trees. Off by the creek, under the cottonwoods, he caught sight of several Indian tepees.

The men coming toward them were a motley crew, unshaven border ruffians. They were armed to the teeth with belted guns and knives, and they looked shaggy and restless. All of them eyed the girl with sudden avid interest.

"When do we ride again, Jode?" The question came from a squat, powerfully built man with a thick black beard. He was ignoring Jackson and the girl.

Jode shrugged. "Two or three days, Matt."

The bearded man seemed disappointed. "I thought that call meant —"

"No new raid," Jode cut in coldly. He put his gaze on the tepees under the trees. "Little Bear back yet?"

Matt shook his head. "Maybe he won't be back." There was no feeling in his tone. "Far as I'm concerned Little Bear an' his smelly braves don't ever have to come back."

"Got a present for him," Jode said. He looked at Jackson and grinned. "You remember Little Bear, don't you, Jackson?"

The Ranger said nothing. His face was tight; it felt like parchment over his cheekbones.

He had lived with the Chiricahuas for five years, but he never felt he owed them anything.

It had been a whim that they had not killed him when they wiped out the Comanche war party and took him along. Lame Coyote had tolerated him, but there had been no love between them. They were Apaches and he was white, and he ran their errands and did their dirty chores around camp with the squaws until he finally escaped and made it to Fort Ivers during one of Lame Coyote's forays away from camp.

Later, as a man grown, he had guided an Army patrol after Lame Coyote, after the Apache had cut a swath through the New Mexican territory. The patrol had finally cornered Lame Coyote and wiped him out.

Little Bear was Lame Coyote's cousin.

Matt was looking at Jackson with new interest. "Jackson, you say? The Ranger Benton was expecting —"

"It's him," Jode nodded. "The girl's Benton's niece. She was nosin' around Dawson's Gulch, so we took her along."

They had moved along while talking. Now Jode dismounted in front of the adobe building. Three men were sitting cross-legged around an old Army blanket spread out in front of the shack, playing poker. One of them said, "When do we get ridin' again, Jode? I just lost my split of that last raid —"

Jode grunted. He turned and searched the men who had trailed him to the building.

"Where's Nat?"

"Inside — sick as a poisoned coyote," Matt

growled. "Cooked hisself a mess of blood sausage he picked up at that Johnson place a month ago. He's lying on his bunk now, green as those cottonwood leaves. . . ."

Jode made a face. "Damn fool'll kill us all yet with his cooking." He looked up at the girl and a glint came to his eyes. He walked over and pulled the girl out of the saddle and swung her around into Matt's arm. "Get her inside. Show her the stove an' where Nat keeps the grub. I want to eat, then I'll grab a little sleep. Someone wake me when Little Bear an' his braves get back —"

Matt smacked his lips. "Never trusted Nat's cookin'. With her around I don't care if Nat never gits well. . . ."

Jackson watched him push Ruth toward the house. He felt despair settle astride his shoulders, but he kept his face bleak and emotionless. He had set a trap, but had forgotten that a trap could spring both ways.

It wasn't for himself alone that he felt trapped. Life had always been a gamble for him, from the day the Comanches had come whooping down on the small ranch on the Salt. But he had not expected Ruth Dillman to be part of this — and he still did not know what had brought her out to Dawson's Gulch yesterday.

Not once during the long night's march had he been allowed to have even a few words with her. She had ridden up front with Lefty and Potter, and Jode had ridden slightly behind him. And he had made no attempt to escape. Jode's blunt statement that the girl would get a bullet the moment he made a suspicious move forestalled any plans he might have made in that direction. The threat had been as effective as a pair of handcuffs.

Jode was looking up at him, grinning. "We've got somethin' for you, too, Jackson. The wheel! Little Bear will like that, when he comes back."

He turned to the men flanking him. "Tie him up! Make it good. Ain't every day we'll have a Ranger on that wheel!"

The wheel was just that, a weathered six-foot rim set on an axle that projected from the cliff. There were dried bloodstains on the spokes and the ground directly under it held the embers of old fires.

They tied Jackson to that wheel. They took off his boots and socks, stripped him to the waist and tied him, spreadeagled, to the spokes. They left him naked to the brutal beat of the climbing sun, to the gnats which swarmed from the stream, drawn by the smell of blood.

They left him there all that day, and at night a guard dozed by the wheel. They gave him no food, but at sundown Jode gave him a drink of water, gripping his hair and forcing his head back while he poured the liquid down Jackson's face. And he laughed while he did it.

"Little Bear should be back tomorrow," he said. "It'll give the boys a change, watchin' that

Apache work on you."

Jackson spat in his face. Jode lifted the back of his hand and wiped away the spittle. Then he closed his fist and sank it into Jackson's bare stomach. He did it twice, then backhanded the sagging Ranger across the face.

"We'll see how cocky you are tomorrow," he snarled, and walked back to the building.

Jackson dozed. He thought of Ruth and put her out of his mind; it only tortured him and he could do nothing to help her. He saw her once; she came to the back door and looked at him. She seemed tired, but there was no sign of abuse and he felt a prod of relief.

He didn't dare think of how long her immunity might last, of what would happen to her when Nat, the sick cook, got well.

But he knew what would happen to him when Little Bear got back. He remembered the runty, flat-nosed Apache with the thick shoulders and thin flanks that gave him the appearance of a copper-skinned hairless monkey on horseback. He recalled that Little Bear had escaped from the San Juan Reservation almost a year ago, and rumor had it that he and the half-dozen disgruntled braves who made the break with him had fled to Mexico.

Jackson had little doubt of what would happen to him when Little Bear showed up. He hoped only that Ruth would be spared the sight.

The night sky dimmed and the stars went out. He dozed through the early morning. His arms were numb. He was awakened by activity around the building. Smoke spumed out of the stovepipe poking up through the roof, and men's voices came loud in the morning stillness. He saw Ruth briefly as she came to the back door and emptied a pot of coffee grounds on a previous heap and went back inside.

The sun came up, moving over the eastern wall of the canyon. His parched lips felt like paper as he ran his tongue over them.

He had guessed wrong, back in Muleshoe. He had let a town force him into an arrogant display of misjudgment. He should have left Muleshoe and filed his report to headquarters, as he had been instructed. But it was too late for such thoughts. And even the knowledge that he knew who the Baron was, and what he was waiting for in Muleshoe, mattered little now.

The guard went inside for his breakfast. Men began streaming out. A few threw him curious glances. But he was Little Bear's prize, and no one bothered him.

The day wheeled through its phases. Once he heard Ruth's sharp outcry, and it was followed by Jode's angry voice. Rage threw him in a brief struggle against the rope which held him. He fought his bonds until his anger spent itself. . . .

Ruth came to the back door later, and he saw the fresh bruise on her face. But there was an undaunted look in her eyes and she held her head high.

She stood watching him for a long time. From

the back door to the wheel it was perhaps fifty feet. Jode's heavy voice called from within. She straightened, raised her hand in a quick gesture to Jackson. It seemed to convey hope, or reassurance. He saw the glitter of a knife for a brief instant before she tucked it back in her dress.

He wanted to tell her that it was hopeless. That she couldn't get within twenty feet of him before someone stopped her. And then it occurred to him that she may have meant that she would use the knife on herself, and the knowledge sickened him.

It was almost sundown when he heard the shout. A man over by the creek was yelling, waving toward the trail.

Jode and the rest of his crew crowded out the front door to watch. From the wheel Jackson could see the riders start down the treacherous trail. He counted six of them, and he knew that Little Bear and his braves had returned.

Even from this distance Jackson could make them out: The half-wild mustangs they rode, the sun on bare copper skins. And though he couldn't pick out features, he remembered Little Bear's flat, ugly face.

The shot seemed to tremble, like a sacrilegious intrusion, on the evening stillness. It was far and faint, yet definite as it came down into that desert hideout.

It puzzled Jackson. But it had more immediate meaning for the warriors coming down into the valley. The end rider tried to turn his pony around on that narrow trail. The lead man, probably Little Bear, was gesturing grimly.

The end warrior suddenly tipped backward, as though pushed by an invisible hand. The sound of the shot came later, as the brave hit the edge of the trail and bounced off the next narrow ledge thirty feet below.

The rest of them dismounted. They tried to shield themselves behind their horses, but the unseen riflemen on the rim were at an angle where they could command all twisting loops of the trail. One by one the horses bolted, some of them tumbling off the narrow trail, dragging their riders with them. Those who got free managed to fire two or three wild shots before they went down before the rifles on the rim.

Jackson surged against his ropes, a wild hope rolling through him like a wave. Judging from the rifle reports, there were at least two men up on that rim, and he had the quick thought that they must be Tom Benton and Marvey Holt.

Jode and his men picked up rifles from inside the building and made a run for the trail. They kept up a fire at the rim, seeking targets they couldn't see, shooting at small puffs of smoke that never rose twice from the same place.

One of the men running at Jode's flank spun around and fell. Jode paused. The others scattered, began to spread out. Their run for the trail dragged.

Out of the corner of his eye Jackson spotted Ruth. She had come to the back door and flung a glance to the men heading for the protection of the trees along the creek. Then she ran for Jackson.

"Ruth . . ." he whispered. "Ruth . . ."

Cold steel brushed his wrists. He felt his bonds loosen, fall away. She bent to his feet. He came free and staggered. There was no feeling in his feet and his hands did not seem to belong to him.

She said quickly: "There's one man in the house besides Nat. If you can get hold of a gun —"

He took the knife from her. It felt big and clumsy in his unfeeling fingers. He started to run for the back door. At any moment Jode or one of those men now occupied with the riflemen on the cliff might turn and spot him.

A rawboned, bald man with a steerhorn mustache appeared at the back door just as Jackson reached it. The outlaw had one moment of startled surprise before the Ranger's hard shoulder rammed into him. He fell over backward and Jackson was on him. The man clawed for his holstered gun, then made a choking, sobbing sound as Jackson's knife reached him.

Jackson grabbed the Colt from his relaxing fingers. Circulation was coming back into his hands and feet. Ruth came in just behind him. She put her back to the wall and slid past the dying man on the floor.

Jackson looked around. He saw that he had entered what looked like a long barracks crowded with bunks. An unshaved man in dirty underwear tossed and mumbled fitfully on one of them. Jackson guessed he was the cook. The man seemed too sick to care what was going on.

He followed Ruth to the kitchen at the head of the building and went past her to the open front door. Outside he could hear the ragged firing as the trapped raiders wasted lead on riflemen they couldn't see. Under a covering fire several tried to make the trail, but each man was dropped before he reached it.

Jode was still by the first tree — a big cursing figure. Finally he turned, and Jackson got a look at his face as the outlaw realized the Ranger was no longer tied to the wheel. He yelled something to the man next to him and came at a run for the adobe building.

Jackson waited until Slade was twenty feet away. Then he stepped out. Jode was half expecting him. He skidded slightly as he twisted and cut down at the Ranger. He fired twice and was himself slammed around by Jackson's two slugs. He fell to his hands and knees and bared his teeth with terrible effort. . . . He tried to get up. Then the life went out of him and he went down hard. . . .

Two others had caught the action. A bullet hammered into the door frame near Jackson's head. He ducked back inside and a bullet screamed through the open door and went through a pan on the stove.

"Get down, Ruth!" he yelled, gesturing grimly. She crouched low by the thick wall and he peered out through the door in time to catch a man running toward the house. He waited until he couldn't miss — The man fell limply.

The others were confused. They were caught between the fire on the rim and that from the house, and they drifted toward the west end of the valley, under the cliff wall, to get away from both.

It was then that Jackson saw Tom Benton. He was a small figure working his way down one of the narrow crevices in the western wall, using a sixty-foot rope to steady himself. He was working his way down to a ledge which bulged over the gunmen at the base of the cliff. They didn't see him.

The old marshal had a small wooden box under one arm. He reached the ledge and carefully placed the box down between his feet.

A straggler down by the creek finally spotted him. He raised a shout and began firing. Jackson saw the bullets powder rock around Benton. Jackson started out the door. The range was too far for a Colt, but he felt he had to do something for that man on the ledge.

Tom Benton did it for him. He drew his Colt and pointed it at the box between his legs. The small gunflash was all Jackson glimpsed. Then Tom Benton disappeared in a thunderous mass of rock and earth that plunged down on the men below.

Some of the debris reached out as far as the adobe building. A pall hung over the piled rubble. Jackson turned and looked back to Ruth who had come to the door. She was staring at that dust pall, a sick horror in her eyes, and he knew she had seen her uncle. And even as he started for her she went white, her knees buckled and she fell.

Jackson picked her up and carried her inside. He put her down gently, propping her up in a sitting position against the wall. She was as limp as a rag. He crouched beside her, suddenly conscious of the heavy stillness outside, pressing down on this lost pocket in the Escalante. Rock dust filtered into the kitchen and he sneezed violently. The move turned him in time to see the figure leaning against the inner door. He saw Nat and the gun in his hand, and the picture of this sick man in longjohns had a ludicrous frame. But the gun in Nat's hand held no humor at all. The muzzle wobbled, and the heavy report sent a slashing pain across Jackson's shoulder muscles.

He fell forward, shielding Ruth with his bulk. He braced himself with the palm of his left hand against the wall over the girl's head and he fired twice under his arm. Nat jerked and fell back out of sight.

The loud reports brought Ruth to. She moaned softly and looked up at him, her eyes dark and afraid.

"It's all over," he said gently. "I think Tom got the rest of them."

She began to cry quietly. He let her be and

walked to the door. He could see a figure standing in full view on the rim at the head of the trail . . . the man ducked out of sight when he saw Jackson.

It looked like the San Saba gunslinger with a rifle in his hands — and it occurred to Jackson now that he still had Marvey Holt to deal with.

He turned back to Ruth Dillman and helped her to her feet.

The sun's rays lay flat across the desert floor. Marvey Holt sagged against the rock guarding the trail, the Winchester he had taken from the dead guard held loosely across his waist. His face was pinched and showed the dark shadows of fatigue. He seemed thinner and older and less insolent, although a trace of the cocky smile edged his lips as Jackson and the girl appeared on the rim.

They faced each other, the Ranger and the gunslinger, and Jackson's hard lips moved in a slow smile.

"You look beat, kid. . . ."

Holt dragged in a long slow breath. "Bone tired," he admitted. He looked at the girl who was staring at the pile of rubble under the western rim. Nothing moved down there, but up in the darkening sky a turkey buzzard, drawn by some mysterious instinct, began a spiraling descent.

"Reckon that's the end of the Baron's dream of empire," Holt muttered. "Caught in their own cul-de-sac." His grin twitched. "Learned that one from my brother, Ranger. Bob was the one with brains."

Jackson relaxed. He felt as beat as this kid, and he was glad he was not going to have trouble with Holt.

"You should have told me," he said slowly, "about your brother."

Marvey closed his eyes. He heard his own cocky voice talking. *"You be righteous, Bob, an' work for peanuts. Risk your neck as a Federal dick. Hell, I'll own half of Brazos County when you'll still be lookin' for money to buy your next shirt —"*

A kid bragging? How much did he have in his pocket right now? Fifty dollars, perhaps. And a gun in his hand —

He looked down at that rifle and then up to the big Ranger. This quiet man had knocked out of his head whatever cockiness he had nurtured concerning his ability with a Colt.

"I figured Benton would head for the desert," Jackson commented. "But how did you find this place?"

Marvey shrugged. "Seems like a nightmare, Jackson. We holed up in a prospector's shack. I was weak as a kitten, but Tom took care of me. That's where he found the dynamite. Then he showed me a note he said Bob had tossed into his office the night Bob was killed. It gave us a clue to getting here." He paused, feeling very tired.

"We might be still hangin' around Skull Rock,

if you and . . . Miss Dillman hadn't come by the other night. Seein' the girl with you an' them raiders seemed to knock the props from under Benton. He just crouched there an' stared into the desert. I thought he . . ."

He didn't want to say it, but the girl said it for him. "Maybe it was better that Uncle Tom went this way. Doctor Harrigan said he would never get well. That at best he might suffer a stroke that would paralyze him —"

Holt stared out into the darkening sky. He didn't want them to see his eyes. He said stiffly, "I never ran into anyone, miss, that I felt I could respect. Until I came to know your uncle —"

He looked down into the canyon; his voice was a low mutter. "We tried to follow you, after. But we lost you. We were wanderin' around out there when by luck we spotted those Apaches. Don't know how we stumbled onto them without them spottin' us first. We had holed up in some shade an' Tom was prowlin' around. They weren't expectin' anyone out here, I reckon. Anyway we trailed them here, saw them hail the guard on this rock. I knew where he was then, an' I got him first off."

His eyes lighted briefly. "We trapped those Apaches on the trail an' got 'em all. Then Tom told me to cover the trail. He disappeared with that box. I thought he . . . Heck, I never figured he'd do what he did."

"He had his reasons," Jackson said. He turned to Ruth. "Feel up to riding?"

She nodded. "I — I want to get home, Jim . . ."

Holt moved away from the rock. His walk was stiff. "I hope I got the man who killed my brother. Those damn Apaches —"

"No Apache killed your brother," Jackson headed him off. "That man is still in Muleshoe." He turned to the girl. "What day was the governor expected in Muleshoe?"

She thought a moment. "Tomorrow. By special stage. He was due at noon."

"Then we should be able to make it back in time." His voice was grim. "Think you can ride all night?"

"I'd want to —"

Jackson turned to Holt. "We'll need fresh horses, water, and I can stand a meal. I think we can pick up what we want down there. We'll start right after. . . ."

XVII

The riders straggled into Dawson's Gulch; they comprised almost the entire male population of Muleshoe. Headed by Phil Petersen and Sam Dillman, they had followed the stage back to the old gold camp — and found George Vollmer's body where Slade had dropped him.

There was no sign of Ruth. Amos Selwick turned a little green at sight of George. Slade's bullets had left the stage line manager unrecognizable.

Sam stared into the dancing heat, his eyes sick. He wondered what he could tell his wife.

Petersen sat tall in the saddle, a commanding figure. His eyes flashed in cold anger.

"I was against him from the start, boys. You all know that. I knew more about him than most of you. Any man who lives with Apaches gets to think like one."

Sam stirred. "We ain't sure of what happened here, Phil. You can't accuse a man —"

"I can and I am!" Petersen snapped. "Hell, use your eyes, Sam! The story's plain enough for me to read here, and I'm no scout. Think back. He talked George into taking the stage out, got himself hired to ride shotgun. George didn't want to do it, did he, Amos?"

Amos nodded slowly. "I heard him ask George — he even promised he'd be responsible for the bullion shipment, in case anything happened."

Petersen laughed triumphantly. "That's the way it was, boys. He talked George into taking the stage out of Muleshoe. And somewhere out of town he put a pistol to George's side and made him swing off the main road, take this road into Dawson's Gulch. Don't anybody tell me George came this way on his own. This isn't the way to Harrisburg, and George knew that as well as any of us."

Men muttered, generally agreeing. The evidence was strong against the big Ranger.

Sam lifted a dissenting voice. "George may have had his reasons for driving up here —"

"What reasons?" Petersen shook his head. "Hell, Sam, I know you're worried sick about that girl of yours. But that isn't any excuse for standing by that renegade Ranger."

Aaron Coots, an oldtimer in the country, had been nosing around. He pulled up by the main group, his eyes curious. "Don't know about that, Petersen. Way I read it, there was trouble here. Four men were waiting up in that oak stand. 'Pears to me Sam's gal rode up here before the stage an' these hombres picked her up. There was trouble when the stage showed up. Somebody fell over here, just past George's body —"

"Hell, you're just guessing, Coots!" Petersen snapped. "Even if it was so, it doesn't mean

Jackson wasn't with them. Because if he wasn't, why didn't he get in a couple of shots at them? Why isn't his body here beside George's?"

Coots shrugged. The others looked uneasy.

Sam Dillman searched those faces and the hope that a posse would try to follow the men who had taken his girl faded. Every man here knew what had happened to Crowley's posse; he saw no desire on the faces of these men to duplicate that ill-fated expedition.

Petersen swung his cayuse around. "Well, let's bring George back. And we'll let the governor worry about this. It's his problem, like I been saying right along —"

Sam was the last to turn away. He was remembering that he had taken Jackson at face value, but the evidence against the big Ranger was bad. He stared off into the glaring distance and wondered where his brother-in-law Tom Benton was, and what was happening to Ruth. He felt sick, and the grayness showed in his face and fear pinched his mouth.

Muleshoe became an armed camp after their return. Several families packed up and left town the next day. The others waited for the governor's arrival with hope and anger. . . .

Sam wakened early on the morning of the governor's arrival. His wife still slept, exhaustion and the medication Doctor Harrigan had given her finally overcoming her. Sam heard the knocking on his back door and went downstairs, a shapeless figure in his nightshirt.

He detoured long enough to pick up a gun and cock it. He was holding it ready when he unlatched the door.

Ruth came in first. He stood rigid, as though a ghost had come out of the pre-dawn grayness. Then Ruth was in his arms, and he heard himself crying.

Behind Ruth, Jackson, helping an unsteady Marvey Holt, came into the room. Jackson closed and bolted the door; he carried Holt to a horsehair sofa dimly seen near the lace-curtained windows.

He told Sam Dillman what had happened over black, biting coffee in the kitchen. Ruth was beginning to relax; her slim body drooped with fatigue. Clara Dillman came downstairs; the reunion was tearful, and after a while the two women went upstairs.

Jackson looked at Sam. "The kid's going to need a doctor. A little rest will fix him up." He drained his cup. "I'm sorry about Tom Benton, Sam."

Dillman was like a man reprieved. He kept rubbing his eyes. "It'll be hard on Ruth, Jackson. She thought the world of Tom —"

Jackson rose. "It'll be light soon. And I want to have a talk with Petersen's printer, Davis. Where can I find him, Sam?"

Sam made a motion with his hand. "Sit down, Jackson. Davis is dead." He waited until the Ranger sank back in his chair. "He was found dead a few hours after you and George left town.

In the alley behind the Oro Grande. Doc Harrington called it an overdose of whisky and a bad heart. Funny thing, though. Doc said it looked like Red deliberately tried to drown himself in the stuff. He had whisky all over himself."

Jackson put his head down on his arms. He was suddenly bone tired. He lifted it a bit to say, "I sort of expected it, Sam. I know now who the Baron is." His eyes closed. "I need a rest. Just forty winks will do. But I want to be up before the governor gets here. It's important, Sam."

Dillman nodded. "I'll see that you are, Jackson."

Phil Petersen left the crowd clustered around the Eldorado Hotel and crossed the street to the *Chronicle.* The midday sun shone on his bared head, on his unruly mass of iron-gray hair.

He walked stiffly, a man occupied with his thoughts, a man turned in on himself. He did not see the tall, broad-shouldered figure who stepped out of the side street and followed him.

Petersen took the long flight of steps alongside the *Chronicle* to his quarters above the shop. He went directly to a trunk he kept in a small closet, unlocked it, picked up a crossbow and two arrows lying on top of old clothes.

He reached the roof of the newspaper building through the skylight. The shop's false front lifted a good four feet above the roof, shielding him from the crowd clustered across the street. He crouched just below the parapet, a tall man nursing a hate six years old.

Governor Coke would be rolling into town any minute now. The special coach would pull up in front of the Eldorado Hotel and he would step out. He would be a plain target for the weapon he held in his hands.

A silent kill!

Long before that crowd realized what had happened he would have hidden the crossbow again and mingled with them around Governor Coke's body.

He waited, nursing his hate.

Then he heard the shouts from below and he knew the governor was arriving. He straightened slowly, lifting the ancient weapon above the parapet. . . .

The voice behind him held a familiar ring. "I wouldn't try it this time, Stafford!"

He stood like a man turned to stone — as if that voice had nailed him to the weathered boards. It couldn't be! Two-Bit Jones had told him Slade had taken Jackson and the girl with him. It couldn't be Jackson!

Below him, the coach, flanked by a special mounted guard, was pulling up to the Eldorado. The crowd moved in around it — but Petersen saw none of this.

"Slade's dead," the voice informed him. "They're all dead. It was a crazy dream, Stafford, your dreams of empire."

"When . . . did you . . . find out?" The words came haltingly, bitterly from the tall man's lips.

"I wasn't really sure," Jackson said. "The clipping Davis lost, something George Vollmer said before Slade killed him. But I wasn't sure until I heard that Davis was dead. I picked up that half-breed Jones this morning. He didn't expect to see me again, so it wasn't hard to make him talk. He'll talk again, Petersen, in front of a jury —"

Petersen whirled. Jackson's shot smashed into his shoulder as the crossbow twanged sharply. The arrow made a thin whistling sound as it went high over the Ranger's head.

Petersen twisted along the parapet, dropping the bow. He crouched like some wild animal at bay, his right arm dangling.

Jackson said coldly: "You'll live to hang, Stafford."

Duncan Stafford, alias Phil Petersen, alias the Baron, shook his head. Jackson was walking toward him when he heaved himself over the parapet. . . .

The Ranger walked to the parapet and looked down on the crumpled body. Across the street, in front of the hotel, Governor Coke, a big man in black broadcloth, was just getting out of the coach. He was twisting, looking across the street, trying to make out what the commotion was about. Part of the crowd, and several of the mounted guard, were headed across the street for the newspaper office.

Jackson shrugged. He picked up the crossbow Petersen had dropped and started back for the skylight.

Solitary Jackson said good-by to Marvey Crane, alias Marvey Holt, San Saba gunslinger. The kid was on a horse, and his hat was tilted forward over his eyes. There was a cocky grin on his lips, but there was maturity in his face.

Jackson handed him the letter he had written for Captain MacDonald. "He'll take you on, kid," he said. "The Rangers need young blood."

"How about you?" Marvey's glance slid away from Jackson to the girl standing in the doorway of the Butte View Lunchroom. He knew the answer, but he asked it anyway.

Jackson smiled. "Me? I'm getting old, kid. I've seen my share of trouble. I think I'll settle down here."

Marvey shrugged. He looked at the badge Jackson had given him; it glittered brightly in his palm. It was something he owed Bob, he thought. That was the way he felt, anyway.

"Well, see you around sometime, Jackson. . . ." He waved breezily, turned his bronc and went up the street, kicking up dust. . . .

Jackson watched him ride out of Muleshoe. He could see the long hard trails ahead of the kid, the disappointments and the dangers. They tempered a man, but Marvey Crane was of the right brand of metal.

He turned and looked at Ruth Dillman and she smiled, doubtfully at first, then more surely as she read his face. He started to walk to her, and his eyes lifted to the desert beginning to fade into the heat haze.

Dull barren hills, burnt hills, ugly hills. Yet there was a beauty to them, too. Some day there would be a railroad through Muleshoe, and the land between here and Concho and Harrisburg would fill up. He saw all of these things in Ruth's eyes, and the hard cold core of loneliness that had been locked in him melted at last.

There was a quickening to his stride as he went to meet her.

The employees of G.K. Hall hope you have enjoyed this Large Print book. All our Large Print titles are designed for easy reading, and all our books are made to last. Other G.K. Hall books are available at your library, through selected bookstores, or directly from us.

For information about titles, please call:

(800) 223-1244
(800) 223-6121

To share your comments, please write:

Publisher
G.K. Hall & Co.
295 Kennedy Memorial Drive
Waterville, ME 04901